SANDCASTLES

SANDCASTLES

❀

part 1

A Novel

Robbie Snelgrove

iUniverse, Inc.
New York Lincoln Shanghai

Sandcastles
part 1

iUniverse books may be ordered through booksellers or by contacting:

iUniverse
2021 Pine Lake Road, Suite 100
Lincoln, NE 68512
www.iuniverse.com
1-800-Authors (1-800-288-4677)

Because of the dynamic nature of the Internet, any Web addresses or links contained in this book may have changed since publication and may no longer be valid.

This is a work of fiction. All of the characters, names, incidents, organizations, and dialogue in this novel are either the products of the author's imagination or are used fictitiously.

ISBN: 978-0-595-44825-8 (pbk)
ISBN: 978-0-595-89142-9 (ebk)

Printed in the United States of America

Prologue

Falmouth Massachusetts

(Cape Cod) February 1999

The young man driving the expensive Cadillac Seville arrives at the entrance of Sandcastles and makes a right turn. He had seen many, many private residential developments in his life time, but Sandcastles was something he was attracted to right from the start. The thought of driving to his future home filled him with great excitement and he couldn't think of a better time to see it than on this cold but sunny morning in February. He is a professional, good-looking man in his middle twenties with dark brown hair that is cut short and crescent-shaped bronze eyes. He is dressed up this morning in his dark suit and tie, and after his visit to Sandcastles, his Cadillac Seville will be back on the highway heading to work. Patches of recently fallen snow are on the houses and properties, and as the young man drives further and further into the development he imagines the kind of beauty a Cape Cod winter will give to Sandcastles. As he drives past the houses he sees recently made snowmen and the footprints of children as they trail through sparkling wet snow. The thought of children puts a smile on his face and he proudly realizes that one of his own children will be brought up in the glorious world of Sandcastles. He has been down these private streets so many times he seems to know where every turn will be before he sees it. On his right and left are beautifully constructed Cape Cod houses, mansions, estates, large and small colonials, tudors, and country-style homes, all built to each owner's specifications. Each street has a long, winding sidewalk and all along the streets are tall lampposts that at nighttime give Sandcastles a pale golden glow. The Cadillac now drives past the recently built condo-style houses made of white-washed brick and clustered together in several rows. He drives down a couple more streets and finally he is at his lot. He parks the car at the curb. They will have several neighbors on this street, but theirs is the last house at the end. The morning is indeed cold and he sees his breath as he stands by his car and rests his eyes on the wooden fountain that sits on their property and will be the home of he and his fiancée. The house will be a large Cape Cod and the beginnings of a garage and family room are noticeable on the right and left side of the house. They will have a large front yard with a long, winding driveway and a large tree shading their home. As he looks at his future house, he realizes how good living at Sandcastles will be for him and his wife and, someday, for their children. Their family will have a wonderful place to grow in, a quiet, upscale neighborhood and a private development with many luxuries such as a private fitness center, playground for children, general store, supermarket, and mini drugstore. As his children grew into teenagers, they and other teenagers would be attracted to the Sandbar, a great hangout for young people. As the young man gets into his Cadillac and heads back to work, he realizes what a great birthday present this will be for his financee. It will be just what she wants, he thinks to himself.

AS KRISTYN LOCKS THE DOOR OF THE Falmouth Cooperative Bank and she and her staff walk toward their cars, the heavily falling snow and wind that whips their faces tells them that the drive home is not going to be pleasant. Kristyn sighs miserably and snuggles more tightly into her lavender winter coat while she waves goodbye to her staff and then unlocks the door to her snow-covered beige Mazda Protege. Sitting in the parking lot of the bank all day, her Mazda is covered in fallen snow and at least ten minutes pass before she is driving out of the parking lot and onto the main road that will take her to her house. She looks out into the March night and sees nothing but swirling masses of heavy snow and winds and people scrambling out into the plaza and rushing to their vehicles. This is definitely going to be the worst storm of the season, she thinks to herself. She looks ahead and very cautiously drives the Mazda slowly down the street, keeping a firm grip on the steering wheel to avoid skidding on the icy road. She is a pretty twenty-two-year-old woman with smooth, silky reddish brown hair that she wears long. Her figure is tall and slender and her large, owlish, light brown eyes are complimented by her light Irish complex—ion and small patches of freckles. Her clothes are smart and sharp looking, and just the right kind of dress for a bank branch manager. If not for the bad March weather, the small house she shared with her father in Falmouth would be easier to get to, and she realizes the slippery streets are going to make the ride home a slow one. She is on a long road now called Old Barnstable. This particular road is very dangerous in inclement weather due to a steep hill that ends with the road being flanked on either side by a cranberry bog. She advances down the long hill and almost makes it to the bottom when the Mazda hits an ice patch and flies out of control! The Mazda is twisting and turning and Kristyn tries desperately to brake and stop the car before it hits an oncoming car. The Mazda hurls forward and crashes into a mound of snow on the right side of the road next to the fence that separates the cranberry bog. Kristyn breathes a sigh of relief and tries to calm her beating heart, which tells her she came very close to a major accident. Illuminated by the glare from the headlights of the oncoming cars, she realizes she has to get out of the mound of snow very fast. Pressing her foot on the gas pedal she turns the ignition on but the Mazda stubbornly refuses to move! More gas and the car remains buried. Angered by her situation now, she slams her hand against the steering wheel. She is stuck. Her first thought is to call her father but when she looks up, a young man is pulling his truck over and stopping. Kristyn rolls down the window and sees a very attractive young man with sandy brown hair and russet eyes. His face is full of warmth and understanding.

"Stay in the car. I'll give you a hand!" He very confidently walks over to the front of the Mazda and begins pushing on the car.

"Put the car in reverse and give it gas!" he orders.

Kristyn does as she is told, while at the same time realizing how enthralled she is with this man who has come along to rescue her. He sure is cute, she thinks. He is pushing on the Mazda with great strength and she is pressing her foot on the gas pedal. She looks through the windshield and thinks of how the whipping snow and high winds must be like sharp knives across his face. After several minutes, he comes back to the passenger side and Kristyn is surprised by the passive look on the young man's face. It certainty looks as if he is enjoying helping her. She studies him more closely now and is deeply fascinated by what she sees. He is like an angel coming out of the darkness to help her.

"Let me get into the car and see if there is something I can do."

Kristyn eagerly agrees and she steps out into the cold night air. He looks like a very skilled driver as he grips the steering wheel and gives the car gas, as he turns the steering wheel sharply to the right and left.

"We're almost there," he says with a smile.

Another five minutes passes and suddenly the Mazda is freed from the snow bank. Between oncoming headlights, Kristyn slowly eases the car out into the street as the mysterious young man watches her closely. There is something about him, she thinks to herself. She feels as if she doesn't want to get rescued out of the snow bank and she would rather stay here with this heroic young man. She turns the steering wheel to the left and slowly begins to accelerate. For a few seconds the Mazda lurches forward and then gets stuck on a small patch of snow. The young man goes over to the back of the car and begins pushing.

"Give it gas while I push!" he orders.

They continue on for several minutes and finally Kristyn steers the car onto a clear patch of road. He comes over to the driver's side window.

"I can't thank you enough for what you did."

His eyes are studying her very closely, and Kristyn is amazed by the look of caring and compassion. It was as if she could look at him in this way all night. "It was no problem at all. Glad to help a lady out."

He makes his way back to his truck.
"Drive safely now."

He smiles once more, climbs into his truck and drives away. Kristyn knew she would not forget this mysterious hero right away. He had been too taken with her. But she would probably never see him again. As she drives down Old Barnstable Road and heads towards home, the cellular phone in her car rings and she realizes it has to be her father calling to find out where she is.

❦   ❦   ❦

June 1999

Kristyn drives her Mazda into the parking lot of the Regatta Restaurant and parks. It is seven o'clock at night and the small restaurant is already packed with customers. She is lucky to get a parking space close to the building. She gets out of the car and looks around. The Regatta is located right at the edge of the water and behind the restaurant is the sparkling blue water of Falmouth Harbor and the Vineyard sound. On the right and left of the building boats of various shapes and sizes are attached to the adjoining dock. The restaurant itself is a small building with a long black roof and white trim. Several windows line the building and flowerbeds rest comfortably on each sill. Realizing she is very late, Kristyn locks the Mazda and hurries inside. She moves quickly past bunches of men and women who are sitting in the waiting area and dressed in their Saturday night best outfits. Waitresses, waiters, and busboys are moving quickly with trays of food and silverware. She scans the large dining room and looks for her party amid the sounds of people eating merrily and indulging in conversation. In the corner of the room, at a large table, she sees her Uncle Curt waving to her and she walks over. She is looking exceptionally pretty tonight. Her freshly washed reddish brown hair is combed and styled. She wears a wine-colored dress that shows off a great deal of her bosom. In her ears are gold earrings and around her neck is a long necklace in the shape of a gold heart. At the table are her Uncle Curt, who is three years older then her, and a group of his friends who he has known since childhood. Her uncle greets her warmly with a kiss and holds out a chair for her at the long table that holds recently poured drinks, bowls of clam chowder, and a large basket of fries. Her Uncle Curt is the first to speak. He is a good-looking young man who greatly resembles Kristyn, with short reddish brown hair neatly cut and light Irish skin with freckles.

"I was getting a little worried about you. I was just going to call the apartment, and then I realized your phone won't be in until tomorrow."

"We had so much to do. There was so much furniture to move. Dad has been great, he and Grandma have been helping me all day long. And even Uncle Charley helped. After they left I had to take a shower, get dressed, you know, the female bit."

Curt laughs suddenly and they look at each other fondly. The resemblance between them is so strong they could almost pass for brother and sister. Curt quickly scans the group of young people sitting at the table.

"Kristyn, you know everybody here, right? I don't think there is anybody here you aren't very well acquainted with by now."

Kristyn looks at Curt's group of friends and they greet her warmly.

"And," begins Curt, "You know the reason we are all here tonight is to celebrate Shane's twenty-fifth birthday, that very drunk clown sitting in the corner."

Shane is laughing in his seat, an extremely handsome young man with small blueberry-colored eyes, neatly cut golden blonde hair, a smooth complexion with a sensual mouth, and a strong, well muscled physique. He could easily pass for a movie star. He holds his glass in front of him and then takes a long sip.

"I am not drunk yet, Curt, but I am getting there slowly. Hey, it's my birthday."

Kristyn looks at Curt's happy and relaxed friends. Tamara Spellman, who is called Tamie, is the warmest and most personable girl of the group. She is fairly short with sensuous electric blue eyes and wispy, bleached blonde hair that hangs down to her shoulders. A dimple sits in the corner of her face and her smile is wide and pretty. Dianne Prescott, a girl who was always in pursuit of Curt when she was young, is average size and has bushy, dirty blonde permed hair. She has hazel eyes, a small nose and wears no make-up and little jewelry. Her attitude is strong and determined. Laura McDermott is a young woman who dated her Uncle Curt for two years in high school. She is the smartest and most intelligent of the group. She already looks like the schoolmarm she will one day be, with her chestnut hair in a bun tonight. Her look is very sharp and observant and her emerald eyes study everything closely. She is quiet and conservative. Tracey Hartwell-Smith is the most interesting of the group. A fairly large young woman, Tracey is a highly energetic and optimistic person with frizzy maple sugar brown hair and pale green eyes. Tracey dated a boy when they all attended Falmouth High School, got married right after high school, and a few years later got happily divorced. Today she is single, an interesting young woman who teaches second grade. David Engstrom sits in the far corner. He is a tall man, six feet, with a wiry body and matted dark brown hair. The quietest of the group, he is an average-looking young man, a physical therapist in Boston.

"We were just about to order but we wanted to wait until you arrived," Curt says.

"And Curt", Kristyn begins, "Not only are we celebrating Shane's birthday but also …"

"Yes," Curt says, "Let's see if Billy Coleman can cut those ties once and for all." Kristyn laughs and soon their waitress comes and they order. After they order Kristyn sits back and watches them as they interact and converse with each other. According to Curt, they have all known each other since grade school and she knows that they are celebrating not only Shane's birthday, but also their move last week into two condos at the exclusive private development of Sandcastles. With her success as a bank branch manager at Falmouth Cooperative, Kristyn is able to move into a condo right next to her Uncle Curt and his friends. Now they all will learn what it is like to be out on their own.

When their meals finally arrive and before they start eating, Curt whispers to Kristyn that after the restaurant they are going back to Shane's house at Sandcastles, a house that is right in back of their condos, where they will surprise him with a birthday cake.

They are all sitting in the great room of Shane's mansion and Dianne looks at the room around her and at Shane. In their group of friends, she probably felt the closest to Shane. Of all their lives, his has been the most traumatic and filled with hard times. To have experienced the deaths of two parents, a grandparent he was very close to, the disappearance of a long lost love and brother leaves a great effect on a person, and Shane certainly showed signs of a hard and difficult life. Caught in situations that he had no control of, Shane grew up in a wealthy family with an abusive and violent father who pushed and over-disciplined him, an aloof and emotionally troubled mother who was an alcoholic and in desperate need of counseling, and an unhappy and materialistic home that was absent of love and security. Mark Daniels, Shane's father, was a brilliant man who owned his own law firm on Cape Cod, and he and his wife Donna built a beautiful mansion in Falmouth with their two sons. Growing up in Falmouth, Shane and his younger brother Patrick were spared nothing materially, but their childhood days were full of abuse and pain. Dianne looks at the great room of the house filled with expensive sofas and chairs, liquor cabinet, wall to wall carpeting, and beautiful paintings, and she realizes that Shane had certainly grown into the kind of young man everyone suspected he would be. He had a gentle and caring soul as well as a great personality that was darkened with loneliness, insecurity, pain, and an addictive and troubled nature. He has turning into everything that his mother was, Dianne thinks sadly to herself. Shane was unable to open his heart and trust other women, and that was the result of women failing him. Sitting in the great room drinking a great deal and laughing with their friends, Dianne wonders if there could ever be one girl who would capture his heart and change him. Building this beautiful and expensive house at Sandcastles soon after his parents were tragically killed in their home by an armed robber and inheriting his parent's tremendous estate was surely a start at finding himself in a hard world that was never kind to him, but Dianne wonders if this was the worst thing that could happen to him now. At the present time, he was a part-time newspaper writer and extremely wealthy and good-looking young man who spent money lavishly on himself and others and who also went from one alcoholic party to another, and also from bed to bed. Dianne gets up from where she is sitting and motions for Tamie and Tracey to join her in the kitchen.

"Let's do the cake now," she says to her two friends.

When they walk into the large white kitchen with the best appliances and kitchenware that money can buy, they ask Shane's young Spanish butler Ramón to help them take the beautifully decorated cake with white icing that Dianne made herself in her uncle's bakery and put it on a large silver moveable tray. A few minutes later the lights in the dining room are turned down low and they are singing happy birthday to a smiling and handsome young man who at the moment is forgetting lifelong problems. Soon after, the fancy chandelier hanging above them is turned back up and the cake is cut. Shane brings out a couple of photo albums accumulated over the years and between mouthfuls of cake they laugh and reminisce.

"Dianne, did you make this cake yourself at the Sweet Tooth?" asks Tamie.

"Yes, I made it yesterday. I even frosted it myself. My uncle has been teaching me so much. I know how to make the donuts, muffins, and I even know how to decorate the cakes."

Dianne looks at Tracey.

"Tracey, by the way, have you come in yet to apply for a job? I'm telling you, while you are laid off from the school, you should work with me there. My aunt and uncle are great to work for, and they can give you all the hours you need."

"I'm still thinking about it," is her reply.

"Look at this picture," Curt says suddenly as he flips through the photo album before him. "This is all of us when we went to water country that summer. I was there, Tamie, David, Laura and Lyle."

The minute he mentions Lyle he regrets it. They all grow quiet as they look at Laura and watch the expression on her face change from happiness to sorrow as she looks at a picture taken many years ago of her and her ex-boyfriend, Lyle Warner. Pain suddenly comes into her emerald eyes and she gets up and walks into the great room. The friends sense the tension of the moment and they quickly change the subject.

"I'm going to clear away some of these dishes," Dianne announces as she picks up a few dishes and heads into the kitchen. Out of the corner of her eye she sees that Shane's handsome young Spanish butler Ramón has the same idea and he follows her into the kitchen. She also sees Tracey going into the great room to talk to Laura. She hears Curt tell the rest of their friends that he sometimes forgets and says things he shouldn't say. Dianne walks into the kitchen and Ramón follows her. José Ramón Santiago, who prefers to be called Ramón, is Shane's recently hired butler. He is a thirty-year-old Spanish man, average height with eyes the color of coal and a dark complexion. His hair is the exact color of his eyes and he wears it long and very close to his shoulders. His face is sharp and sinister and he sports a thick goatee. He is dressed in dark pants and a white shirt and tie, the kind of dress required of employees in Shane's home. Dianne had met Ramón a few times during his short employment at Shane's house. She regarded him as a very quiet and suspicious person who couldn't be trusted. She also found him to be extremely attractive.

"Well, that was some cake you made in there," he says. His coal-black eyes stare at her closely as he puts the dishes on the counter.

"Thanks."

"We should put you on staff here. Shane and everybody else around here will be eating very well indeed."

His voice is strong and masculine.

"Well, I already have a job, two jobs, and I am not looking for another," Dianne says with a smile and begins to put the dishes in the dishwasher.

"Yeah, and we already have more help around here than we need. But one more female around here wouldn't hurt at all."

Ramón stares at her and Dianne feels the shock go through her. He is flirting very seductively with her and it makes her heart pound with erotic pleasure. But there is something about him. And she has a steady boyfriend. It also wasn't hard to figure out she was the reason he had come into the kitchen.

"Excuse me, I have to get back out there."

She walks out of the kitchen and he leans on the counter and watches her with a grin on his face.

❦   ❦   ❦

Ramón looks out the window of his bedroom and watches Shane's friends as they head back to the condos that are right next to the backyard of his house. Their laughter and chatter disappears as soon as they turn the corner. He snickers when he turns away from the window and kicks off his shoes and falls onto the bed. What a day, he thinks to himself sleepily. The friggin guy is going to work me like a damned dog. But not for long. He had only been here for a month and had already come to the conclusion that Shane Daniels was a money-hungry self-centered slut who only cared about himself. And he had never met anybody as neurotic and troubled. The guy definitely had some serious issues. During the day, Shane made him responsible for the cleaning, management, cooking, and outside work of the house, which required the services of two other part-time cleaners and cooks and one part-time gardener. The whole house is one big joke, Ramón thinks miserably to himself as he looks around the room that Shane gave him, along with a private bath and private phone line. Ramón came to the conclusion also that he detested the guy's friends as well as the household staff. If they had Shane for a friend there was definitely something wrong with all of them. But Dianne was different. He was attracted to her from the moment he saw her. And he knew tonight that she was just as attracted to him as he was to her. The fact that she had a boyfriend meant nothing to him. He had been in this situation before and he always managed to get a girl to weaken for him. Our day is coming, that is for sure. His eyelids were getting heavier and heavier and he felt sleep coming upon him. He would have fallen asleep right away if the phone next to his bed hadn't started ringing suddenly. He listened for his voice on the answering machine and listened to the message.

"Ramón, hi, it is your mother calling you. I found out last week that you are living here at Sandcastles. And you know that I am living here, too. I have been trying to get you all week. I know you have been getting the messages and I really need to talk to you. If you could, call me back at the number I am going to give. Please son, don't ignore me. I am your mother. I want to talk to you."

Ramón is wide awake now and staring at the phone. The woman's voice is filled with a great deal of sadness and pain and she leaves a phone number for him to call.

"You are not my fucking mother."

He says these words suddenly with a great deal of anger and tries to go back to sleep.

❦   ❦   ❦

Rosalinda Fitzpatrick, who prefers to be called simply Rose, puts the phone back on the receiver and stares at the phone. Going over the events in her mind she is suddenly filled with an uncontrollable sadness and tears spring into her eyes. She places her hands up to her face and before she knows it two large tears begin rolling down her face like slowly poured maple syrup. She is a beautiful fifty-year-old Spanish woman with light brown hair and Spanish coloring. She resembles her son Ramón with the same cue-ball shaped eyes and strong Spanish nose. She wears many rings and bracelets and a gold necklace, a present from her third and present husband, hangs around her neck. Tonight she is dressed in a light blue nightgown. She hears footsteps coming into the foyer and her husband Christopher Fitzpatrick stands by the phone next to her. She looks up at Chris, the best thing that ever happened to her. Her strength, and salvation. Most people would regard him as a fairly good-looking, forty-seven—year-old man with dark hair, dark mustache, and athletic body, but to Rose he was the most indescribable and beautiful man she had ever known, inside and out.

"Did he talk to you?" he asks quietly.

"No," she says with a sigh. "Your loving stepson and my first-born son is not going to give in so easily."

She clenches her hands into fists.

"I wish I could just go over there! It is so frustrating. We live in the same damned neighborhood! But I don't know that guy he works for. And he is not going to give his mother a hug and kiss when he sees her, that is for sure."

He warmly touches her side and she falls into his arms.

"Give him time. He will come around. Once he sees that you really care about him." Rose wasn't so sure that was ever going to happen.

Kristyn has just put on her pink nightgown and is sitting down to relax on the new sofa that sits in front of the TV. Going over the events of the day she realizes how much she has accomplished. She is finally settled in her new condo and she can live her life without worrying about her overprotective father. Just thinking about her father makes her sigh with exhaustion and she wishes more than anything that he would find a nice woman and stop worrying about her. But he is not all that bad either. As she rests her head on the white sofa, she reflects about how her birth must not have been an easy time for him.

Her mother, Theresa, and Bill had been high school sweethearts and her mother gave birth to her in their senior year. It was agreed that Kristyn would live with her mother and Bill would help support the child, and then suddenly, Theresa and her parents had moved away and did want to have any contact with the Coleman family. Theresa had given Kristyn to Bill for the day and never returned. The Colemans just assumed that Theresa had made a terrible mistake and wanted to begin a new life, at her parents' urging. So Bill Coleman became a father at age seventeen. Kristyn was just one more member of the already growing Coleman family due to the fact that the two brothers already had a three-year-old brother named Curtis. And so Kristyn grew up in the Coleman family household. Charley eventually went away to college and Kristyn was left in the care of her father, uncle, and grandparents. Right from the beginning, Bill was overprotective and eventually her grandmother, Carolyn, became equally overprotective. Curt and Kristyn grew up like brother and sister and eventually Bill got a good job and was able to live in a house with his daughter. There had been a few women in his life, not many, and Bill centered his whole life around being a devoted father. Sometimes too devoted. He was always too worried about her, even if she only left the house.

During her girlhood days Kristyn didn't mind it too much but during her teenage years she resented his strict and smothering ways. Her grandmother was just as bad but she didn't live full-time with grandma. She ended up going to college on the Cape where she could commute and soon after got the job at the bank. She worked hard and saved her money and a few months ago decided her father was going to have to cut the ties and let her live on her own where she would find the peace she was always looking for. She was proud of her newly rented condo and Bill was somewhat glad Curt and his friends were living in the building right across from hers.

Her cellular phone rings and she is suddenly jolted out of her relaxed state. She goes to pick it up, knowing already who it probably is.

"How are you making out? Is everything okay?" the male voice asks.

"Dad, hi, you woke me up. I was just about to turn in."

She was hoping her father would take this as a slight hint.

"Boy, we sure worked hard today, didn't we, Kris? All that furniture that we moved. But we had help, too, with Grandpa and Uncle Charley. Is everything hooked up? Are you completely settled in?"

"Everything is great. In fact, everything is so great, I am just about to turn in. Curt and I had a great time tonight at Shane's birthday party."

"Alright, I'll let you go. Remember, don't open up the door to strangers, don't give your name over the phone, and—"

She finishes his words. "If I need anything important, Curt is right across from me."

She has barely a couple of minutes to rest her head again on the sofa when her doorbell rings. Not expecting any company at this hour, she walks over to the window and by the light of the lamppost, she is able to make out a young man, a young man who looks totally unfamiliar to her, yet she realizes she has seen this man before and knows it is perfectly safe to open the door.

She opens the door and a flood of memories come flashing back. The sandy brown hair, the great body, the russet eyes. The man who helped her push her car out of the snow. The young man begins to speak and then a twinkle of recognition comes into his eyes. He recognizes her right away. Kristyn is the first to speak.

"Hi! Remember me? You helped me get my car out of the snow last March!" Not that she needed to tell him all over again. As they stand in the doorway she wonders what he is doing at her door late on a summer night.

He begins to laugh and they feel warm and at ease with each other.

"Hi again! Well, well, it certainly is a small world, isn't it? It has been a couple of months since I helped you, hasn't it?"

"The March snowstorm," Kristyn replies with a smile on her face, still wondering what he is doing here.

He is still grinning when he begins to speak to her.

"I was just about to go into my condo when I noticed that your headlights were still on. At first I didn't know whose car it was, even though the Mazda looked very familiar. I know everybody's car around here, even the new guy who just moved in across from me. I figured it had to belong to the new girl who moved in today."

"My headlights? Oh my goodness, that is right. I put the lights on earlier when I was in my car and forgot to turn them off. Oh, how silly of me. Thank you for telling me."

She looks at him again and her heart is bursting with happiness.

"Your condo? You live here?"

"Yes," the man replies, and begins pointing.

"I live in the condo right next to yours. We are neighbors."

Kristyn is speechless.

"Let me walk you to your car so you can turn those lights off. You don't want to wear down your battery. By the way, I am Darren, Darren Lane. And you are?"

"Kristyn, Kristyn Coleman."

They leave the condo and walk to Kristyn's car.

❀   ❀   ❀

Laura comes out of the bathroom she shares with Tracey in their rented condo and sees Tracey lying on their couch watching TV.

"What's on?" Laura asks. She is washed up for the night and is wearing a long white nightgown. She has let her chestnut hair out of the bun and it hangs full.

"ER," Tracey replies, "I couldn't see it the last time it was on, so I taped it."

Laura laughs and says, "At least now I won't miss my shows because you will always have the VCR taping them. What's after ER?"

"You know, it's funny. I watch soap operas, and I sometimes feel my bad marriage to Todd couldn't compare to some of the stuff they go through."

Laura starts laughing suddenly.

"Yes, but at least your marriage lasted longer than some of theirs."

"You have a point there, teacher."

"I'm all done in the bathroom. You can go in now and get ready," Laura says and settles down on the couch.

Tracey gives her a worried look.

"What about you? I was worried about you tonight. As soon as Curt brought up Lyle, you seemed to get real upset. Does the break up really bother you still?"

Laura's reply is strong and firm.

"No, I am over Lyle now. For years I was deeply hurt by it, but it just wasn't meant to be. If we went through all that we went through in college, god only knows what our marriage would have been like. And he is somebody that will never change, believe me."

"Alright. I am going into the bathroom to wash up."

Tracey goes into the bathroom and Laura is left alone watching TV. Moments later sounds of running water come from the bathroom. Laura can't stand the temptation any longer. The thought was on her mind after she saw his picture and even when she was in the bathroom. At first she dismissed the thought and then she realized that she had to know. Hearing his voice again certainly wouldn't be a good thing to hear, but she has to know if he is still living at the same house in Easton, Massachusetts, the place where they went to school together. She reaches for the phone and stops to remember the phone number that she once knew by heart. She dials the number and listens to the rings. Somebody is picking up.

"The number you are tying to reach, 1-555-1001 has been changed. The new number is—"

Laura hangs up before she hears the number. Her curiosity is satisfied. He has obviously moved and is established somewhere else.

"Hey, Tam, is that popcorn almost ready? We are starving in here!" Curt shouts.

"Almost ready!" she shouts back. "I just have to pour the butter over it."

Tamie laughs and picks up a pan of melted butter and pours it very generously over two large bowls of popcorn. Dianne suddenly appears in the small kitchen the four friends share and helps her bring the bowls of popcorn into their living room. David is sitting very quietly on the couch and Curt is sitting on the sofa chair next to it. The TV is tuned into MTV and Curt is laughing at what he sees on the screen. When the girls come into the room the men turn their attention away from the TV and grab handfuls of the popcorn. The two women sit down on the couch next to David and begin eating as well.

"I don't know how we can eat after all that cake at Shane's house." Dianne says.

"I don't know about you guys, but I can eat popcorn anytime of the day," Tamie says between mouthfuls.

"Me too," Curt says.

"And me as well," David says.

"What did you guys think of Shane tonight? Did he get wasted or what?" Tamie asks.

"It was a good thing he wasn't driving home from the restaurant tonight," Dianne says.

"Yeah, by the time we left the house tonight, he was getting pretty wasted," David says.

"Any more and that creepy butler of his would have had to carry him up to his bed. There is something about that butler I don't trust," Curt says.

"I don't think Shane trusts him either. I mean I know Shane very well and all, and I just have that feeling," Tamie says.

Dianne stops eating her popcorn suddenly and glares at her friends.

"We should stop making fun of Shane. We all know the reason he acts the way he acts. The way he drinks and all. He is just escaping."

They all agree and for a few moments eat their popcorn in silence. While she is eating her popcorn an idea comes to Tamie suddenly. She tells her friends she has to make a phone call and hurries up to her room. While she is going up to her room she hears Curt ask Dianne if Tracey is going to work with her at the Sweet Tooth. It was agreed that she and Dianne would have one phone line and David and Curt would have another. The great benefit of their condo was that each of them had their own room. Tamie picks up the phone and lies down on her soft pink bedspread. She does not remember exactly this particular phone number so she dials information and then dials the number. A young male voice answers.

"Hello?"

"Justin? Hi, it's your cousin Tamie. Tamie from Darlene's wedding today?"

"Tamie, wow, I didn't think I would hear from you so soon," the astonished male voice replies.

"Justin, I know it's late and I hate to call you and your mom so late, but today, at the wedding, when you two were leaving, your mother dropped her wallet. I saw it fall to the floor, and by the time I picked it up, you two were already gone. I know how important a wallet is to a woman, believe me. Has your mom said anything?"

"Tamie, I don't think she has even noticed yet. She hasn't said one thing. Did anything fall out?"

"No, everything is all there. I have it here, in my room, and I can bring it over first thing tomorrow morning."

"Do you remember how to get to Sandy Neck beach? Do you need me to give you directions? I know you haven't been here in a while."

"Oh no, I know how to get there, Justin. I used to babysit you when you were little, remember?"

Justin laughs.

"Yes, only I am not so little anymore."

"No, you're all grown up now, I'm afraid."

There is a moment of silence and then Justin speaks.

"Tamie, my mom and I had so much fun with you today at the wedding. It has been a while since we all have seen each other, it was so good to catch up."

"Yes, and we are going to see each other more often. We are family, and our mothers have always been close."

"Yes, blood is thicker then water, Tam."

"Tell Marie that I will be over sometime tomorrow morning with her wallet."

Darren and Kristyn sit on the wooden bench that is placed right between their two adjoining condos. The courtyard is beautifully constructed with red brick walkways, patches of freshly cut grass, colorful beds of flowers, and brightly lit tall lampposts, which, at this hour, provide the only light. The light from the lampposts also makes the several condos in the courtyard very visible and all around them they see small beautifully built buildings made of white washed brick with long sloping roofs, one, two, or three windows, chimneys on top, and trimmed bushes in front of the condos. Kristyn looks at Darren. He is the most fascinating man she has ever met, and a man she knows her father will approve of right away. She has never had a lasting relationship, and she suspects Darren Lane might well be the first. Darren seems taken with her as well. They have been sitting on a wooden bench that is placed within every two condos and for a long time they have been talking and laughing. At the moment they are holding each other close and staring into each other's eyes. Kristyn looks at the condo that is placed in front of Darren's.

"Who lives in that condo?" she asks as she points to it.

"A young guy who moved in a month ago. He is from Easton. Nice guy. We have really gotten friendly in the time that he has lived here. Lyle is his name."

"Well, Lyle is Lyle, but I think I prefer the guy next door," Kristyn says suddenly, and she is shocked by her bold words. She has known this man less than two hours. They look at each other with a great deal of passion and then their lips meet. To Kristyn it seems as if their lips were joined together for the longest time and then they pull back from each other.

"Well," she says, "You have told me everything about your life, where you have been brought up, what you have done, and I have told you the same, but, what happens after being a grocery manager?"

He stares at her and his face is ignited with passion.

"Oh, you know the old bit, marriage comes, and then a house, and then babies. Of course, tonight has made me think of all those things greatly."

They take each other's hands and hold them firmly. For a few moments they are silent and stare up into the clear night sky that is filled with stars and constellations.

He looks at her again.

"When we left each other the night of the snowstorm, for a long while after I couldn't stop thinking about you."

Jogging is the exercise she enjoys the most and on this beautiful and clear Sunday morning in June, Julianne Lincoln, a pretty twenty-three-year-old who prefers to be called Jill by her friends and family, works up a light sweat by jogging around Sandcastles and greeting all the neighbors she knows very well. She knows it is all part of her personality and spirit and Jill can't think of a better way to treat people then to bring out the good in them. She stops jogging when she reaches her driveway and walks slowly into the house she shares with her mom and dad, two brothers, and one sister. She is dressed today in a light navy blue top and shorts and white sneakers. Her long and full strawberry blonde hair hangs almost down to her waist. She is an average-size young woman with a petite figure. She has large cornflower blue eyes and her healthy complexion is complimented with bright rosy red cheeks. She moves very quickly into the house. It is a large Cape Cod house with several bedrooms upstairs and a wide and spacious front and backyard. Her father built this house many years ago when Sandcastles was in its early development. From where their house stood, Jill and her family could easily view the Fitness Center, one of the most popular establishments in Sandcastles. The aroma of chocolate chip pancakes fills her nose when she walks into the kitchen and her mother Christina asks her if she will be joining the rest of the family for breakfast. Jill tells her mother she is skipping breakfast and goes right into the living room and picks up the phone. She dials the very familiar number and waits for him to pick up.

"Hello?"

His voice isn't the cheeriest this morning but he seems to be alert and awake. "Hi hon, how are you?"

"Oh Jill, how good of you to call."

She can picture him smiling on the other end and it fills her with a great warmth.

"You sound like you are a little sick. Is everything alright over there?" she asks him.

"Oh yeah, everything is just fine. Just a little hung over from last night, that is all. We celebrated my birthday last night, and then they all came back, and we had a few drinks."

"You don't have to say anything more, hon. It is your birthday. You're supposed to have fun on your birthday."

"Thanks, Jill."

The young man she is talking to is her close friend and Sandcastles neighbor Shane Daniels. They had met a year ago when Jill was jogging past his newly built house and their friendship had grown stronger ever since. They were two people who could totally understand each other without saying a word. They shared many of the same interests and were bound together by strong ties of friendship. In the year that they had known each other Jill had considered him to be one of her best friends. They could call each other at the latest time of the night and talk for hours and hours. Another reason she was so drawn to him were the many factors and past events he had experienced in his lifetime that had deeply effected his soul. She considers him to be one of the nicest people she could know, yet as nice as he was, she knew from the way he talked about his life that all his past experiences had him constantly wondering who he was and where he was going in life. Her training in psychology and love for this particular friend has given her the initiative to help him as best as she can.

"Hon, do you have plans this morning?" she asks him. "It is absolutely gorgeous out. We should go to the beach and get a nice tan."

He laughs at her use of words and she is noticing that the hangover he had prior to talking to her is fading slowly away.

"My friends and I are all going to the beach. Why don't you come along, Jill? I talk about you so much and they would love to meet you. We're going to the Falmouth beach."

"Oh, I am so glad that I am finally going to meet them, and since they are living behind you now, I should be seeing them a lot."

"Throw your suit on and be over in a half an hour."

"Oh Shane, before we hang up, I have the funniest story to tell you. Stephanie and I were at the Sandbar last night, and we, actually I, met the funniest, weirdest guy. He is a Spanish guy, and the funny part of it is, I actually gave him my phone number. Wait until you hear this story."

On Saturday nights the Sandbar is a very busy place, and when Jill and her friend Stephanie walked in, Jill wasn't surprised to see the dance floor filled with young people and people at the bar seated almost back to back. She looked very pretty tonight. Her strawberry blonde hair was long and flowing and she had faint touches of make-up on. She was dressed in her casual Saturday night clothes. Her friend Stephanie, a non-Sandcastles resident, was shorter than Jill and had shoulder-length brown hair and large glasses. Going to the movies was out of the question. They had seen everything playing. To be sitting inside Jill's house was not an idea that particularly thrilled both girls, and Jill suggested that they visit the Sandbar. It was a great place to meet guys and Jill knew many of the young people from the neighborhood would be there. The Sandbar was a large building and it offered the choice of a sit-down bar, restaurant, dancing, and an arcade with video games.

"You are so pretty!"

Jill looks into the face of a young man who is obviously of Spanish descent with Spanish coloring, light brown hair, and light brown eyes. His dark pants are clean but his white shirt is torn and grubby. He grips a cigarette in his fingers.

"Excuse me?"

They had been sitting on the barstools sipping drinks and talking. Out of the blue, this strange Spanish man appeared and his gaze was fixed directly on Jill.

"Hey, how ya doin?"

The cigarette comes up, he takes a quick puff and blows the smoke in a different direction.

"Been watchin you for a while now, and damn girl, you don't look like you belong in a sleazy place like this bar."

At the end of his words he gives a short laugh.

"My, my, aren't you quite forward," Jill says, still very mystified by this man. "I live in this neighborhood and Steph and I decided to stop in."

"Cool," he says with a wide smile on his face, "I'm Ricardo Antonio Lopez, and everybody calls me Rich. You looked very interestin and I just had to come over and see who you was."

Jill was beginning to feel more at ease with him and although she introduced Stephanie, she was the one he was most interested in.

"So you live in Sandcastles, huh? That's funny because I pretty much know all the chicks around here, and I ain't seen you yet. My ma lives in Sandcastles. I do, too, on this side of the street, and my ma, Rose, lives in a mansion on this side, too. I live in the condos right across the street from here. Girl, I gotta sit down and rest my tired feet."

He sits down on the vacant stool next to Jill and puts his cigarette out. Jill begins to tease him.

"Maybe that is the reason you don't know me. Old Barnstable Road divides Sandcastles into two parts, and I live in the other part. Maybe you need to get around more."

He laughs and when he laughs his face takes on a very comical and happy look. She could tell he was a man who enjoyed great humor.

"I never visit people in the other section. They are much to lame for me."

He signals to the bartender with the snap of his fingers.

"Bartender, could you pour me a Budweiser? And two for my lady friends as well."

Jill and Stephanie spent the rest of the evening at the Sandbar, and Rich Lopez spent the rest of the evening next to Jill. In the short time that he was with her, she learned a great deal about him. His mother Rose was a wealthy woman who lived in Sandcastles. He shared his condo with his friend Eddie. He had brothers and sisters who still lived at home. He has had more jobs then he could possibly remember. He was currently employed at the Falmouth Burger King. He was twenty-six years old and had no motivation or desire to be anything in life. To be in the company of this strange man was not what Jill planned for tonight, and despite the fact that he was different then her, she couldn't help but be attracted to him as well. He could sense this attraction and played upon it.

"Girl, before you leave here tonight, you have to give me the number to your pad."

They had just come off the dance floor and were headed to their table in the restaurant section. Stephanie was seated at the table and looked very lonely waiting for them. Jill looked at him. He was like a strong magnet and she couldn't say no.

❉   ❉   ❉

Dianne adjusts the straps on her two-piece black bikini and puts on a white top over it. She is ready for the beach and can't wait to lie on the sand under the sun. She begins to pick up her beach equipment, towel, chair, radio, and book, when she sees Tamie saunter down the stairs and head into the kitchen. She asks her friend why she is not dressed yet for the beach.

"Oh, I can't go this morning. I have to stop off at my parent's and then I have to stop at my cousin Marie's house. I have to bring back the wallet she left at that wedding yesterday."

Tamie goes into the kitchen and begins taking items out of the refrigerator and David and Curt happily trail down the stairs with their bathing suits on and towels in their hands.

"I'm surprised Shane is even going to the beach this morning. He probably has the worst hangover," Curt says.

The three friends laugh and step out onto the courtyard. It seems as if people in the condos farther down the courtyard have the same idea and they leave their small houses in bathing suits and carry beachwear. Standing a few feet away from them are Laura and Tracey, dressed in their bathing suits as well.

"We just have to go and get Kristyn. She wants to go too," Curt says.

They head toward the condo and when Dianne looks in back of her, she sees her long-time boyfriend Jon Canter walk over to her condo and knock.

"Guys, go on ahead and I'll meet you at Shane's. Jon is at my condo."

This was totally unexpected. She wasn't planning on having him show up. And in a normal circumstance, he would call her first. Any irritation she feels, though, is washed away when she greets her dark-haired, pale-faced boyfriend with small beady eyes at her door.

"Honey, you didn't call me and tell me you were coming over. What's up? We are all heading to the beach. Do you want to join us?"

The expression on his face tells her that he is not here for happy conversation.

"Dianne, you and I need to have a talk."

"What is wrong?"

"What is wrong? What isn't wrong!"

The next couple of minutes are spent with him demanding to know why after four years she is suddenly pulling away from him, looking for a way to make her life more meaningful, and shacking up with her friends in a expensive rented condo in the most expensive area in the whole damned town.

"Jon, we have been over this many times." He throws his hands up in the air and very angrily walks around in small circles. "Is it me? Am I the reason you are doing all of this? What do you want to do? Call it quits after four years?"

"No, Jon, darling. You aren't the reason. The reason is me."

She walks over to him and plants her hands lovingly on his shoulders.

"My house is too small. With my sisters there, there is hardly any room. With all of us living here, the rent is hardly anything at all."

"We agreed that you would stay home until we got married. That is where I want you to be!"

"I need to do something with my life! You have a great job, you have done this and that. Jon, I need to do something different with my life, and this has nothing to do with you. I need to work myself into a career. A career is something that I have never had. Just part-time jobs. I bake pastries and then I help women try and fit into clothes. And this move is a great change. I just want to feel useful and important. I have plenty of time to do all of this. When we are married, that is a different story, but please, have faith in me and be patient."

He turns hurtful eyes towards her.

"I don't know, Dianne. You are just not the same anymore. You haven't been the same since you moved in here. It is like you are pulling back from me. I just hope that rich friend you have living behind you isn't influencing you in some kind of way."

❦   ❦   ❦

From where he stands at the top of the stairs he can very easily see Dianne as she walks across the lawn up to the front door. His mouth waters when he sees what she is wearing beneath the white top. Except for Donna, the cleaning lady who is working in the room down the hall, he is the only person in this part, and it is a perfect time to see what is going on without being noticed. Below the second floor, Shane and his stupid friends all dressed in their wimpy bathing suits are in the kitchen and he can hear their talk and laughter. If it weren't for him, useless Shane would still be in bed sleeping right now. Dianne looks troubled, too. Her face wears a mask of frustration. He knows exactly what would take the frustration right out of her. Dianne walks up to the front door, lays her beach wear on the marble floor, and prepares to walk into the kitchen, when Ramón walks down the flight of stairs and greets her at the bottom.

"Mighty hot day today, isn't it?" he asks very nonchalantly.

Dianne's hazel eyes sparkle with interest and excitement.

"Depends on how you look at it. In your situation all you have to do is loosen that shirt. We, on the other hand, can relax and feel cool on the beach."

He laughs and it is a cold and chilling laugh.

"I always liked a girl with a great face, great body, and great sense of humor."

"Do you want to come join us at the beach, or, are you hard at work here in the house?"

"No, I am on duty right now. Some of us do have to work for a living around here. But, after work I was thinking about shedding these clothes and jumping in that pool out there in the backyard. Are you sure you don't want to take off that top and join me? I sure would love the company."

His voice is a low and sexy whisper. They stare at each other and their passion boils like a volcano about to erupt.

"I'm glad Shane pays you for more then just trying to seduce his friends," Dianne says and heads towards the kitchen.

❦   ❦   ❦

Lyle opens up the door to his condo and steps outside. The day is beautiful, he thinks to himself, but when he breathes in the Cape Cod air, the feeling does nothing for him at all. In fact, it only makes him more miserable to think that he has to live in this part of the state when he could be back in his hometown of Easton. An idea comes to him and he begins to walk to where his red Mustang is parked in the parking lot. He is a very tall man, nearing six feet, and three words that come to mind for any woman when she sees him are "tall, dark, and handsome." Lyle has neat and trim ash-black hair and ash black eyes. His complexion is milky white and smooth and he has a small and firm mouth. Before him now is the hose that the development offers the tenants to wash their vehicles. Lyle unwraps the long hose from where it is placed and examines it to find out how it is turned on. He turns the knob on the faucet and still no water comes out. Suddenly, a long gush of water spurts his face and his clothes and he angrily throws the hose on the ground, where it once again sprays him in the face. Behind him he hears a male laughing and he rushes over and turns the faucet off.

"There is a trick to that thing. I have to show you how it is done."

Lyle looks up as Darren walks over to him.

"Sorry, but I didn't bring my towel," he says and bursts into laughter.

Lyle smiles at the sight of what he has just done and begins ringing his blue shirt out with his hands.

"This kind of thing happens to me all the time. I never thought moving out on my own was going to be this difficult. Last night I almost burnt the condo down with a fire that started in my oven. I sure do miss my mother's cooking."

"But you are on a mission here, and that mission is to find your ex-girl-friend," Darren says.

"Yes, but finding her is going to be like finding a needle in a haystack. I know she is not living at home and if her old man catches me anywhere near the house, he is going to go inside and take out his shotgun. She could be any-where."

Darren laughs and tries to soothe his worries. Since Lyle had moved into the condo in front of him, the two men had begun a friendship and seemed to share many of the same interests.

"I take it you had a good time last night," Lyle says, "I saw you and that girl who just moved in sitting on the bench. You two were out here for the longest time."

"Yes, she is at the beach right now. Let me tell you, man, this girl is terrific. I helped her out in the bad storm we had last March. We hooked up on our first night together. The only downfall is she has a very overprotective father and an overprotective uncle who lives in the condo in front of hers. Her old man probably is not going to like having me around. She is daddy's little girl."

"Her uncle is one of those kids that live in that condo? That is funny. I haven't even paid attention to those new tenants. I am always so busy. I never have time to go outside the condo. The commute to Boston to work easily takes up so much time, and my mind is constantly thinking about Laura and where I can look to find her."

"She will show up real soon, I am sure."

❧   ❧   ❧

Tamie drives her gray Toyota Corolla down Sandy Neck Road. Up ahead in the distance she can see the glistening blue waters of Sandy Neck beach. The area and the homes are absolutely breath-taking, she thinks to herself. It is no wonder her cousin Marie and her second husband were so happy here. Being right next to the ocean surely gave them the most invigorating air and breath-taking view. Tamie glances down and looks at what she is wearing. She definitely is not dressed to go swimming in her cut-offs and light cotton shirt, in case Marie invited her to go down to the beach with her. Although she can't explain to herself why, she is taking one hand off the wheel and pulling off her engagement ring and sticking it inside the glove compartment. She also can't explain why she is glancing in the rearview mirror and making sure not a hair of her bleached blonde hair is out of place. She has even put on a little lipstick. The Toyota pulls up to an old-fashioned blue Cape Cod-style house with white trim and a small garage off to the left. Two high windows are placed in the sloping black roof and a small white fence surrounds bushes and small beds of flowers. The small street has just a few other houses on it and for a backyard Marie and her family have the private end of Sandy Neck beach for their enjoyment. Tamie parks out front and walks up to the front door and is greeted by her mother's first cousin, Marie. Marie Dehanley, married a second time after her first marriage to Robert Riley ended in divorce, stands before her with a happy expression on her face. Marie is thirty-nine with shaggy titian hair that leaves her with high bangs across her forehead. She is very tall and slender with a long neck, small nose, and apple-green eyes, the color of Justin's. Tamie can see the many resemblances to Justin, as well as to her own mother. Resembling her father more in looks, Tamie likes to believe that it is her mother and her mother's side that she takes after the most. They greet each other warmly, even though it has only been a day since they last saw each other and caught up with each other's lives.

"Here is your wallet. Good thing I saw it. You wouldn't have wanted Aunt Stella to pick it up. You might have never have seen it again."

"Oh, Tamie, thank you so much. You are a doll! Come in. I was just about to sit down to a cup of coffee, and now you can join me."

Tamie walks inside the house. In the dining room there is a sliding glass door that leads out to the deck and beyond that the beach. She can make out the figures of a young man and dog running up and down the beach and she realizes who it is.

"Please don't mind the house, Tam. I know it is a mess," Marie calls out from another part of the room as she tries to make her house look clean.

"But that is what happens when you have an eight year- old and a twenty-year-old at home. John went to pick up Melissa at a friend's house." She rejoins Tamie in the dining room.

"Is that Justin out there?"

"Yes, Justin and Nakita, our chocolate lab. Go out and say hello to him, and then come back in and we'll have some coffee. I should have asked your mother to come over."

He looks like any other young man on a beach, but to Tamie the sight of her grown-up cousin takes her breath away. Yesterday he was dressed very formally in a jacket and pants and this afternoon Justin Riley looks very casual in light cut-off jeans, sneakers without socks, and summer shirt. His young, strong body radiates with adolescence as he throws a stick into the surf that crashes onto the shore. Nakita the labrador runs happily into the water and retrieves the stick to take back to her master. She runs back to her master and drops the stick by his feet.

"Good girl! Good girl, Nakita."

Off into the distance, the sun is beginning to set in the clear blue sky and Tamie can smell the strong, salty ocean air. A few seagulls are coming down and resting very near to Justin and Nakita.

"Tamie, you're here!"

He turns around and once again she is looking at the light apple-green eyes, light color, frizzy nutmeg hair, and innocent boyish expressions. She has seen these traits ever since he was a young boy, but now, he is different. He is a man now.

"I didn't hear you come in. This is great. I hope you are staying awhile. My mom and I would love the company."

Even though they are third cousins, the way Justin looks at her sends shivers down her spine. He looks at her in a soft and gentle way, a way he has never looked at her before. There is desire in his eyes and makes her feel warm and happy, yet at the same time a little frightened.

"Of course I am staying. How often do we get to see each other? And we are family right?"

"Let's take a walk down the beach. Come on, Nakita."

Brian lays flat down on the lounge chair with his feet up. He never felt as relaxed as he does right now. But of course, he works hard for it all week and a Sunday afternoon by the pool is like heaven to him. He looks over at his fiancée Karin as she lays next to him on a towel.

"More suntan lotion, sweetheart?" she asks him.

"Little more."

She gets up off the towel and a few moments later he feels the cool liquid being rubbed all over his back. Soon the rubbing stops and they are doing their best to soak up as much of the sun's rays as they can before it sets. He sure is lucky to have her. Brian Olson is a twenty—five-year-old CPA and the head of his accounting firm in Boston with a head full of wispy dark brown hair and crescent, bronze eyes. He is a husky man, almost six feet, and when he is not relaxing by a poolside, he has the look of a first-rate professional with his business-like clothes and courteous professional manner. Working hard and striving for what he wants is the driving ambition behind Brian's spirit, and this driving spirit enabled him to move fast in his career and achieve great success. His fiancée next to him is twenty-five-year-old Karin Lee Griffin, a strikingly beautiful woman with full red lips, soft and smooth black hair, large prominent nose, and brown eyes. They have been engaged for exactly two weeks and have been going together for the last two years, since the end of a previous bad relationship for Karin. Brian looks at Karin very closely now and is so glad that he moved out this way after being a resident of Rhode Island. Brian met Karin at a New Year's Eve party two-and-a-half years ago and for the last two years he has been blissfully happy with a woman who understands him to the fullest. He left his small apartment in Rhode Island to come and be with her on the

Cape and at the present time he lives in a apartment in the town of Bourne, right next to Falmouth.

He is suddenly bolted right awake when he feels two large hands tip his lounge chair over and send him right into the water! When Brian reaches the top of the water he looks at who his attacker is and relaxes when he sees one of his good friends, Curt Coleman. Karin and Curt are laughing and Brian takes his arm and splashes Curt's dry clothes.

"I owe you for this!" Brian yells out and soon he is back on the cement.

"I just had to do it, just had to do it," Curt says as he tries to stop laughing. Karin throws Brian a towel and Brian dries himself off. Brian looks around him. They are at Karin's house in the backyard of Karin's pool with nobody home but the three of them. Out in the distance the sun is slowly setting. Brian and Curt have been friends ever since college. They met at Roger Williams College when they were freshman and through the years managed to keep in touch with their other friends from college as well. Curt knew he was going to be Brian's best man and was awaiting the announcement any day.

"We just came back from the beach," begins Curt. "The whole group of us. I saw Brian's car parked outside and I thought I would stop off and visit."

"Well, we are glad that you did," answers Karin. "Would you like to stay for supper tonight? I am cooking a big meal for my mother and Brian."

Karin's voice is as lovely and sweet as birds singing in trees and Curt looks at her fondly, approval for their relationship in his eyes.

"Oh, thanks, but we had so much stuff at the beach. Thanks for the offer, Karin."

She accepts his apology with a bright and cheery smile.

"Well, Curt, Karin and I have news for you. If you don't have any big plans this Christmas I would like for you to be the best man at our wedding."

"You guys finally got …"

"Engaged!"

Both of them say it at the same time, "Honey, take Curt up to your room and show him the ring."

Rose can hear the sound of his slowly dying station wagon a mile away, and when she looks out the window in the living room of the mansion, her suspicions are correct. She watches her second-born child, Ricardo Antonio Lopez, struggle greatly as he tries to get out of a station wagon that is badly in need of repairs. The windshield has many cracks in it and has spray paint all over the front. It is also without hubcaps. Watching her son from the window, she puts a hand to her mouth and holds back laughter as she watches him finally get the door open after several minutes and walk towards the mansion. Rose looks all around the white living room with the soft wall-to-wall white carpeting, fancy chairs, bar in the corner, and heavy satin drapes and she decides this will be the best place for them to talk. While Rich is walking to the front door of the mansion, Rose wonders what she will say to him as she walks through the foyer to greet him. She also wonders if there will ever be any hope for him. He is twenty-six years old and his life is indeed a mess. She opens up the heavy oak door and then ushers him inside the mansion. She plants a light kiss on his cheek to show her affection and signals to him with her hands to be quiet as she throws open the heavy white doors to the living room and they step inside.

"How about, 'Hello Rich, nice to see you today, my favorite son. It is so great to see you. I think the sun has followed you inside.' Every time we see each other, Rose, our greetings are always the same. What is wrong with this picture?"

Rose sighs deeply.

"Oh, Richie, please, not today. Something terrible has happened, or is happening I should say. I am not in the mood for your dry humor."

"What is wrong, Rose? Why are we in this room anyway? Why don't we talk out in the kitchen, like we always do?"

"Your stepfather is sleeping and I don't want our voices to wake him."

Rich looks at his mother with great annoyance and reaches down into his ripped pants with many holes and fumbles for a cigarette in one of the pockets.

"Richie, no, not here, not in my house. Chris wouldn't like it and I don't like it either. If you want to smoke, go outside, or do it in your own condo, please."

"Chill, Rose, just chill yaself down, girl. No harm done."

Rich and his mother are silent for a moment. "Where is everyone?"

"Mari is at a friend's house, Carmen is shopping and Jim is at a softball game."

She looks at her son with worried eyes.

"What is going on with you? I will tell you my bad news in a moment but I want to hear from you. How are your bills? Are you paying everything on time? How is the condo?"

"Everything is alright, not great. Eddie is having a hard time paying his half of the rent, which is typical of him. I have so many bills, and there is never enough money. Burger King is going to have to be it until I find something else. Last night I was out partying. Met a girl. A real nice girl, too, pretty and all. I'm gonna go after her, too. I partied so late last night I overslept and came into work late and all. An hour late."

"Rich! How many times do I have to tell you. You can't go into work late! That is so irresponsible. One of these days they are going to fire your Spanish ass and then what will you do then?"

"Chill, Rose, just chill yaself down, girl."

Rich looks at the pained expression on his mother's face.

So, what's the bad news?"

"Your half-brother Ramón is back in town."

"Ramón is back? In Falmouth?"

"Yes. He has been back for quite a while. He is working as a butler for a wealthy young man living here at Sandcastles. His name is Shane Daniels."

"You should call him up and see him. You haven't seen him in years. Are we gonna see him, too? Has he chilled out yet?"

Her eyes begin to fill up with tears and she looks away from Rich.

"That is just the problem. You know how things are with my first-born son, the son that I gave to other people to raise because I was young and I made the wrong choices."

"He doesn't want to see ya?"

"No, he doesn't want to see me. If he wanted to see me, he would have seen me by now. He acts like he doesn't even have a mother. And he does have one. He has a mother who after thirty years still loves him very much."

The afternoon sun is dipping lower and lower behind the ocean far away, and off in the distance the sky is emitting faint rays of reddish yellow light that lightly bathes the waters and beach of Sandy Neck. Off in the distance and away from the Cape Cod house Justin, Tamie and Nakita walk slowly down the beach made up of soft sand and small clusters of seaweed. Neither of them were in any great rush to get back and while they are walking and exploring the beautiful Cape Cod scenery, they feel wonderfully at ease with each other. Tamie looks at Justin and wonders how many hearts he has broken and will break in the future. There is something magical about him, and for the last two hours they had explored almost the entire length of the long beach that extended out to the Barnstable Harbor. During this time the boy she had always known had grown into a very sharp and intelligent young man who was kind and terrific fun to be with. Off to the right stood the high dunes of Sandy Neck with tall grass that swayed in the wind and Justin would throw a stick and they would laugh when the eager and energetic Nakita would run into the dunes and fetch the stick for her master. While they walked along the beach, Justin talked about what was happening on the Cape and Tamie sensed he wanted to spend some time with her away from Sandy Neck. They are almost at the house now and Tamie can make out the figures of Justin's stepfather, John, and little sister, Melissa, sitting on the deck and waiting for their return.

"Are you hungry?" Justin asks her.

"Starving."

"Why don't we go and get a bite to eat at Seafood Sam's down the street, just the two of us."

"You have a date there, little grown-up cousin of mine."

His apple-green eyes twinkle with excitement.

❧   ❧   ❧

"Jill, telephone!"

They are all sitting in the living room of her house watching TV on the large set. Seated on the couch is her father Gene and ten-year-old sister Elizabeth, and on the opposite couch next to her are her two brothers, twenty-seven-year-old Billy and nineteen- year-old John. Her mother is cleaning up the kitchen and the phone has just rung. Jill walks into the kitchen and sees the phone lying on the counter and realizes that her mother must have gone into another part of the house.

"Hello?"

"Jill, whatcha doin girl?" asks the very familiar voice. Remembering the previous night puts a smile on her face. Jill is expecting this call.

"Rich, how are you? I was expecting you to call me but I didn't think it would be tonight."

"I can't help it. I miss ya babe."

They make small talk about their day, the night at the Sandbar, and then Rich comes right to the point.

"Jill, I get outta work at Burger King at five. Why don't ya swing by? I'll show ya my pad at Sandcastles. I would even like to show you to my ma. She would luv ya. I even asked her to have dinner with us there. She is mighty rich, let me tell ya, and my step-dad is cool, too. How about it?"

Jill's reply is yes right away, and after they hang up she ponders on her decision. What is the matter with her? To be in the company of this man excites her and terrifies her at the same time. In another part of this neighborhood is a man who couldn't be any more different from her. Her mother will never approve. Except this man has endearing qualities that seem to go far past his many faults and Jill knows that is the reason she is becoming so taken with him. As she leaves the kitchen she silently hopes that there are enough decent qualities in Rich Lopez to overcome the huge doubt that she has about him.

It is Tuesday evening and Jill sees an empty parking space at the Falmouth Burger King and drives her red Honda Accord coupe between the yellow lines. She has just gotten out of work at Picture Perfect, the photo lab in Falmouth where she works, and as she looks in the rearview mirror she decides to herself that her appearance, make-up, and hair are just perfect to please Rich Lopez. She hurries up to the building. Before her is a Burger King that looks the same as any other Burger King, and at first glance, she takes the male clerk sitting outside the curb as any other Burger King clerk, and when she looks again she realizes it is not just any other clerk but her date for the evening. When he sees Jill he puts the cigarette he is smoking on the pavement and crushes it with his foot. He gets up and smiles at her. He is dressed in the required colorful uniform and still wearing the same torn and dirty pants. His face and hands are greasy.

"Hi! You are right on time. I was just smoking a butt here to pass the time. I have to change, but I can do that at the condo. We should probably take your car, since mine is slowly dying."

They open up the door into the condo and step inside. On the way back to Sandcastles the suspicions that are brewing in Jill's mind are confirmed. She knows Ricardo Lopez is a good-hearted young man and good friend who only wants to do good in a world he cannot take seriously. He talks to her as they approach the small, white-washed brick, one-room condo on the other side of Sandcastles.

"Jill, your friend Stephanie, what a lame gal she is. You have to have more exciting friends! Boring! A night with her and I would fall asleep before eight."

They walk inside the room and Jill's thoughts from a moment ago are suddenly erased from her mind. The young man with long brown hair that hangs to his shoulders with an unkempt moustache is obviously Eddie and they are interrupting him as he takes a small pipe and breathes in. His eyes are red and swollen. Lost in his own world, he barely looks at them when they walk inside the condo. Lying on the long countertop are stacks and stacks of dirty dishes and pans. Near Jill on the coffee table are ashtrays with at least a dozen cigarette butts. The linoleum floor in the kitchen area is splattered with streaks of dirt. On the floor in the living room area are bunches of dirty clothes. On the couch are several dirty socks.

"Eddie and I were going to clean today, but we didn't have time. Sit down, Jill." Smoke. As Jill breathes in she suddenly smells smoke! Suddenly, they see smoke slowly seeping from the oven!

"Eddie!" Rich screams.

Panicked, Rich runs over to the oven, takes out potholders and opens the oven door. A burst of smoky air hits him in the face and suddenly the whole room smells of smoke. He takes the remains of charred pizza out of the oven as a panicked Eddie comes running over. Rich throws the burnt remains into the sink and quickly turns on the faucet. The pizza recoils in a sizzling wet steam.

Rich is enraged and Jill is doing all she can do without laughing at the two men.

"Eddie, what the fuck are ya doin! I told you to watch the food when it cooks! There could have been a big-ass fire in here!"

Jill suddenly feels the need to interrupt.

"Rich, what time did your mother say she wants us at her house for dinner?"

Tamie walks down the stairs and just as she reaches the bottom there is a knock on the door and Curt is walking over and greeting their caller.

"Shane, come on in, man."

Shane walks in and greets Tamie and Curt who are facing him and Dianne and David who are sitting on the couch watching TV.

"Guys, I just want to let you all know there is going to be a big party at my house this coming Fourth of July weekend Saturday. I am going all out. There are going to be tons of people there. I am inviting people from the neighborhood, friends of friends, you all can bring whoever you want to bring. It starts at seven. And the word to pass around is bring your own alcohol! Not that I won't have a ton already at the house."

Tamie smiles and begins to walk out the door.

"Boy," Shane says, "Don't you smell good tonight. I almost want to take you home with me."

"No thanks, you aren't my type," is her reply, and before she shuts the door she tells her friends she is going out with her fiancée, Keith, for the evening. She feels bad because she knows she is telling a lie, and she silently prays that Keith does not call her tonight.

They pull up to the tall, two-story brick mansion in Jill's Honda Accord coupe and when they step out, Jill hopes that Rich's mother is going to be nothing like him. The disaster at his condo seems to be forgotten and Rich is once again in a cheery and happy mood. How bad can she be if she lives in this beautiful house, Jill thinks to herself.

"Ya gonna luv ma. And they'll be no burnt pizza in this house. Ma and Chris get waited on by the servants."

"The rainbow. We have to go on the rainbow!"

"Are you sure you aren't going to be too scared?"

"Course not."

They were at the Barnstable Country Fair in Falmouth, a fair so large it seemed everyone on Cape Cod came to see it. Located in a grassy open area not far from Old Barnstable Road, the fair on this balmy summer night in June is filled with dozens and dozens of Cape Codders from young and small to middle aged and elderly. The shrieks of children can be heard as the many rides of the fair twist and turn at unbelievable speeds, go up and down, or send the children upside down in a splendor of fun and excitement. Those who don't care for the rides can take their chances and bet at the many games that line the midway. Hungry appetites can be satisfied with large and deliciously moist stacks of fried dough that are sweetly dripping with confectionery sugar. The scents of furry animals, haystacks, snack bar food and many different kinds of people fill the air, and there is a complete atmosphere of warmth, families, and friendship.

Justin takes hold of Tamie's hand and holds it firmly. Caught up in an intense emotional moment of confusion and betrayal, she cannot believe she is not letting go and for the first time, she simply does not care. They have walked the entire fair at least two times and now they are walking slowly and aimlessly with their thoughts on each other as they try and comprehend the whole situation. Tamie knew this situation started Saturday at her cousin Darlene's wedding and had been building slowly ever since. As happy as she was holding her cousin's hand and pretending very well there is no blood relation between them, Tamie couldn't think about what this could do to her upcoming marriage of one year, her friends, and her mother's family. I'm happy, Tamie thinks to herself, and yet I feel so confused. She looks at Justin, a boy she saw playing with trucks and bulldozers many years ago and now a young man who stands inches taller then herself. He is looking at the skydiver ride that is shooting mini cars up into the summer night and she notices how different he is from Keith, her boyfriend of five years and to whom she is currently engaged. Keith is older, more distinguished, with streaks of gray already in his hair at twenty-nine, and a totally different personality than Justin. Poor Keith, Tamie thinks to herself. How completely devastated he would be if he knew what the girl of his dreams was doing with her third cousin. Although she has not worn her sparkling engagement ring since Saturday, she knows Justin is aware of her engagement, even though neither one of them is bringing it up. Over and over again in her mind she keeps asking herself if her lack of love for Keith is making her do this or if there is something else. Keith is so good to her. Keith! He is standing a few feet away, with two of his best friends, at a betting game. She remembers him now telling her on the phone he was getting together with Paul and Chet this week but she didn't expect them to come here! She is going to get caught. They are just about to turn around and head in her and Justin's direction.

"Justin, come on, we have to get out of here, fast!"

As they walk quickly away she briefly explains to him what is happening. She turns around. Near her the young men are quickly advancing and Tamie believes no one has identified her yet. What will they do? What will she say to him? 'Hi, Keith, this is my cousin, we are dating!' Without hesitating, Tamie points to the rainbow ride that is letting people on, and after they fumble for their tickets, they step onto the platform and get buckled in. The ride remains on the ground and she winces in pain as at first the men go by the ride, and then suddenly they are curious and decide to wait in the line. Neither of them have seen Tamie and Justin and just when she thinks for sure Keith is going to identify her, the ride leaves the ground and goes higher and higher into the air. Beaten at her own game, Tamie begins to sob.

"They are going to see us!" she screams to her cousin who is buckled in beside her.

He lays a comforting hand at her side.

"No they won't. When we land we will sneak out the back and over the fence. We can do it. Remember what we keep telling each other, blood is thicker than water!"

Comforted by his words, the smile returns to her face once again. A memory that she will never forget as long as she lives is when Justin unbuckles his seatbelt on the great and dangerous rainbow and with more bravery than she has ever known, he walks from his unit to her unit as the rainbow reaches its highest peak. He is in her unit now and when she unbuckles her belt they become one on the ride, caught in each other's arms, their bodies holding tight, the wind whipping in their faces, and their lips finding a safe haven.

The Sandcastles private Health and Fitness Center is a two-story building that offers a variety of programs and exercises, and to Kristyn it seems as if there is too much to do—free weights, racquetball courts, rowing machines, and Stairmaster machines, as well as the exercise bikes and treadmill. She and Laura are dressed in their sweattops and shorts and are looking forward to working out together in the large facility. The two women come out of the locker room located on the first floor and begin to walk to the weight room.

"I am so glad I have someone to work out with," Kristyn begins. "It is so much more fun and the time passes much quicker."

"I know what you mean," Laura replies. "It gets you much more motivated when somebody is working along side with you."

The two women sign in at the desk and make their way over to the gravitron, an exercise machine used to strengthen the upper body. Laura goes on first, and with her arms she pulls herself high in the air with the help of a moveable platform. Up and down she goes with her well-exercised body aiding her to endure more and more high pull-ups. Now it is Kristyn's turn. Much taller then Laura with long arms and lean figure, Kristyn hoists herself high in the air and manages to come up way higher on the bar then Laura. Interested in a piece of equipment a few feet away, Laura walks away from the gravitron.

Kristyn is just about done now and is preparing to get off when Lyle comes from another section of the gym and walks by the gravitron.

"Lyle, this is a surprise!"

"Hey, Kristyn, I didn't know you were here tonight. Is Darren with you, too?"

"No, he is home."

Lyle is dressed in very sexy athletic clothes and wears a white towel around his neck. He is sweating profusely.

"Did you come alone?" Lyle asks her.

"No, I came with a friend. Actually, I should have you meet her. She lives in the condo right near us. Let me go and get her."

Lyle waits patiently by the gravitron and Kristyn walks over to where Laura was just standing a few moments ago. She is gone. She must have gone to go look at something else or is upstairs.

"Lyle, she was just standing here a second ago, and now she is gone. Sorry, I was hoping you would meet her."

"Don't worry about it, I have to get going anyway. If she is living in that condo I am sure I will meet her soon enough. See you around, Kristyn." He waves and then is gone.

      🍁   🍁   🍁

"I like her, Rich. I like her very much."

They are having dessert in the dining room. A large white cloth covers the dining room table and two candles burn brightly next to a pot of fresh flowers. Above them, a three-piece chandelier burns brightly. On the table are apples and cream cake topped with cool whip. Saucers of coffee are around each plate and a pot of coffee sits in the middle of the table. Jill has gone into the bathroom to freshen up and Chris has gone into his office for a moment. Rich and Rose are left at the table and are commenting on how the night has been.

"Rich, if you lose her, you are a damned fool. It is very obvious that she likes you, but she said to me earlier that she couldn't understand your lifestyle. And I cannot understand it either. Impress her. Fix yourself up. Stop wearing those grubby clothes, get rid of that piece of junk car, get out of that apartment and get yourself a decent job! She is the first girl you have ever cared about, and—"

Rich interrupts her.

"Wait a minute, Rose. You are sayin do this and do that. I want Jill to like me for me. There ain't nothin wrong with my life. I just don't have all kinds of money to impress her. And she likes me for me. If I go and change myself and end up lookin like all those goody-two-shoes wimps with no balls, then she ain't gonna like me for who I am anymore. The first part about likin someone is acceptin who they are."

"How does she know Ramón? I heard you two talking about him earlier."

"She is good friends with the man he works for, Shane. She couldn't believe it when she found out me and him are half brothers. She says we are totally different and that is true. That guy needs to chill himself down. He got a serious problem."

Rose puts a loving hand on her son.

"Richie, if you ever do see Ramón, just be nice to him. If you think we had it bad all those years that we struggled when you were growing up, think of how bad he had it. Your life was a fairy tale next to his, believe me. I don't blame anybody but myself."

She feels her eyes beginning to moisten and she hopes she can have at least one night when she won't cry herself to sleep over her first-born child.

"At the time, I thought I was doing the right thing for him."

"It has been so long since I've seen him. Think he was sixteen or seventeen. I won't recognize him when I see him."

"You will. You will know exactly who he is when you see him."

Livvy, their maid, comes into the dining room.

"I hate to bother you, Mrs. Fitzpatrick, but you have a phone call. The caller says it is urgent, and he won't leave his name."

One more annoying thing he has to do tonight, and then he can turn in. To call this particular house annoys him more than he could ever explain, and he is going to make it short and sweet.

"Hello?"

"Mrs. Fitzpatrick, I have gotten your messages and tonight I am putting aside time to answer them."

Ramón, please don't call me Mrs. Fitzpatrick. I am your mother, your only mother."

"You are not my mother."

There is a terrible silence between them and then Ramón is the first to speak.

"Look, this is not a social call. I have gotten your messages, and I don't want you to call me anymore when I am here. I don't want to talk to you anymore either. That part of our lives is dead now. You have your life and your money, and I have mine. A life that is all because of you. So stay away!"

She is sobbing now.

"Ramón, I know I made terrible mistakes. But please, give me a chance. That is all I am asking. A chance. I love you just as much now as I did when you were four. You loved me very much back then, and I loved you."

To hear her words puts an aching and a longing inside of him and for a moment he is taken by everything that she says. And then it hits him.

"You should of thought about the consequences of your actions back then," and then he hangs up.

❧   ❧   ❧

Working with Tracey at the Sweet Tooth had been the only positive part of her day, and when she stops to think about it, the only part of the day that made her happy. Accepted as part of the team, her uncle hired Tracey as a full-time clerk and throughout yesterday and today Dianne tried to show her and teach her as much as she could. Working together would surely be fun and the two girls had almost matching shifts throughout the week. As much as she enjoyed the bakery, though, Dianne knew it was high time to go out and do something much better. She drives her Ford Escort down Old Barnstable Road and through the Sandcastles entrance, marked with a huge stone sign with the inscription "Sandcastles" and different sized boats engraved into the stone. Patches of green grass and flowers decorate each stone and they give the development a nice appearance. She very angrily puts her foot on the gas pedal and controls the wheel as she remembers how bad her day was. Everything had been going great until she went to the Dress Barn that night. Now she has one job when she used to have two. She parks her car in the usual parking space and when she looks up she sees Jon at the door waiting for her. Their relationship has been getting steadily worse and Dianne wonders if they should take some time apart from each other. Jon is right. She seems to be slowly pulling away from him. He follows her happily inside the condo, and seems to forget anything that might be negative in their relationship.

"I don't work at the Dress Barn anymore."

They are sitting very quietly on the couch, and although it is Thursday evening, nobody is in the condo except for her and Jon.

"What happened?"

"A lot of it they say is my attitude, and I think they are right. I don't really know what I want. They told me I could quit, but my hours at the bakery are taking up way too much of their time, so now I will be working fulltime in my uncle's bakery with Tracey."

She begins to look at Jon.

"You know, Jon, maybe you are right. Maybe what we need is time apart from each other. Do our own thing for a while. Not totally break up, but take some time to find out what we want and where we hope to go."

Next to her, Jon is looking at her with a painful expression and she realizes right here and now she has really hurt him.

"Is this what you want?" he asks her.

"I think it is for the best, at least for a little while. You keep making the claim that I am pulling away from you and maybe that is a sign that we both need some serious time apart."

"Alright, if that is what you want, if that is what will make you happy."

A few minutes later they are both silent as he walks out of the condo and shuts the door.

❈   ❈   ❈

The crash of the waves as they hit the shoreline is like several hands clapping together suddenly, and is really the only noise they hear, except seagulls lingering in the distance. Twilight is coming slowly to Sandy Neck beach and the sun forms a soft reddish ball that is dipping behind the ocean. They walk very slowly in their shorts and tops, barefoot, hands held tightly together. In the gentle wind Tamie's long blonde hair sways softly back and forth.

"I have to tell him."

"Yeah," Justin replies, "I think it is about that time."

They are the only two on the beach and off in the distance Tamie can make out the lights burning brightly in Justin's house.

Tamie feels tears coming on strong and her words suddenly feel choked and hard to get out.

She clutches Justin's hand tighter.

"The thing is," she says, "I don't know how we are going to pull this off without hurting people in the process. I just can't go on with Keith. I did have feelings for him, but when you find the right one, it's different. And what about our families and friends? I have been lying all week and telling my friends I am going out with Keith. They don't even know about you."

"We are going to have to keep it a secret for a little while longer until we work out a solution," he says.

"I am going to have to tell Keith. He is starting to suspect something is wrong. I know him. This week I have been very distant and he is starting to notice."

"My mom and step-dad are beginning to notice how much time we spend together, too. Before, we were just two cousins who for the last couple of years had only seen each other at weddings and holidays."

"My friend Shane is having a big Fourth of July party at his house Saturday and Keith is going. Why don't you go, too? I want you to come. I certainly won't have a chance to tell him anytime before that. You will just be a cousin I have invited."

"I will bring a friend, too, so no one suspects anything. Sooner or later we are going to have to find a way to let people know what is going on with us."

❈   ❈   ❈

The chicken had a little longer to cook and the peas and mashed potato were warmly sitting in their pans on the stove, so Kristyn put down her cooking utensils and joined Darren in the living room. While her boyfriend of one week sits on the couch and watches TV, Kristyn snuggles up next to him. Darren's eyes are glued to an episode of the show "Friends." While they watch, he grabs her hand and holds it tightly.

"Supper almost ready?"

"Almost. The chicken has a little longer to go. And then after that, I made you a dessert, but I want to surprise you."

"Your dad doesn't like me."

Kristyn looks at him in surprise. Her father had only seen him twice this week and Kristyn hadn't noticed any—thing too suspicious. He ran distrustful eyes over him, but Kristyn knew the thought of any man coming into her life would make him very cautious.

"Oh, he doesn't even know you yet. Give him time. Once he gets to know you, he will warm up to you, believe me."

"I just get that feeling. Like he doesn't want me around you. Thinks I am no good for you."

Another thought comes into Kristyn's mind.

"What do you think of Lyle trying to find that long lost girlfriend?"

"He is bound and determined to find her. She is not at home, and he is calling up friends they had in college to track down her whereabouts. He keeps getting a cold shoulder. He believes she could possibly be a part-time summer teacher at Cape Cod College and he is thinking about going over there and tracking her there. I guess the break up they had in college was pretty bad, and a lot of people turned against him. Laura is her name."

Kristyn sits up quickly on the couch and stares at him with wide eyes.

"Laura is her name? Laura?" she repeats. Darren nods his head.

"Where did they go to school together?"

"Stonehill College, in Easton."

"Darren, she lives next door, she is one of the girls in that condo!"

Darren's face is full of shock and now it becomes clear to the both of them. "Are you sure?"

"Yes, it has to be her. At first I didn't put two and two together. Laura next door is an old friend of my uncle Curt's, and mine too, now. She dated my uncle in high school and after that she was with a guy named Lester or Larry, something like that when she attended Stonehill. Now I remember, his name was Lyle. They have been broken up for years. At first I didn't make the association between Laura and Lyle, but it has to be them. I didn't think an old boyfriend of hers would show up on the Cape. Stonehill is where they were together. I almost introduced them Tuesday night. We are going to have to tell Curt to keep this a secret until we find a way to have them meet up."

"She might not want to even see him," Darren says.

Before they can say anything more the doorbell rings and Kristyn goes to answer it. Both of them look annoyed. They weren't expecting any company.

"Dad! What are you doing here!"

Darren whirls around on the couch and Kristyn opens the door to let in her father, a thirty-nine-year-old man very much resembling Curt, with reddish brown hair and a mustache, as well as her grandmother, Carolyn, an older woman with large glasses and beautifully styled, dyed white hair. For a second, Kristyn is speechless as her father and grandmother survey her. Her grandmother smiles warmly and her father runs cautious and distrustful eyes over the condo and the young man sitting on the couch.

"We were in the neighborhood, and we just wanted to stop by and see how you are making out. Seeing if everything is okay," her father says.

"Well, I was right in the middle of—"

"Making supper!" Grandma shouts and walks over to the oven.

"Oh look, Bill, she even knows how to cook for herself. Grandma taught you well dear, that is for sure."

Darren walks over and her father very coldly greets him.

"Since we are here, we might as well stay for a while," her father announces as he goes to sit down at the kitchen table.

"Gee, Dad, Darren and I were just about to sit down to eat," Kristyn says.

"Oh, don't be ridiculous Kristyn, you two kids go on and eat." Grandma giggles as she looks carefully at the room around her. "Your father and I ate and we don't mind dining together with you and your friend. Besides, we have nothing better to do tonight anyway, right, Billy?"

"That's right," he answers. "Just want to see how my daughter is faring."

"Kristyn, you know what," Grandma says, "I have been looking around this room and you and I are going to have to get together and set a time when I can come over and help you decorate. Wait until you see what I can do to your condo, sweetheart. I will have this place looking like the president's suite!" she exclaims with excitement.

Kristyn walks slowly toward the oven, and the anger is burning inside her like an uncontrollable fire.

"Oh, this is so much more fun than watching TV," Grandma says.

Ramón walks into the Sandbar and is glad that on Thursday nights the place isn't so crowded. He needs to sit down and have a nice long drink by himself and try to sort out everything that is happening in his life. He is very close to quitting his job and moving off, somewhere far from the Cape where he wouldn't have to deal with his mother's guilt and her useless attempts at trying to win him over. Over the years when he was growing up, he had put up with her phony phone calls and his meetings with her and her children, but now he felt enough was enough. To work in that house all day long was another situation that he was growing tired of. At first when Shane hired him, he thought he had struck gold. The kid seemed like an easy enough target, and he believed that in due time he would let his guard down long enough for him to make his move. But Shane Daniels was certainly keeping a watchful eye on him and Ramón knew he had to be careful. His only real reason to stick around is Dianne. Tonight he had even gotten to kiss her when she made the phony claim she was at the house to see Shane. Just thinking about her gave him an aching and burning sexual desire and he is glad that the alcohol will quench the sizzling sexual feeling he feels inside of him. It won't be long now, he thinks to himself. Two or three times with her and then he will be on his way. He looks around the room. A couple of people sit in the restaurant section and a few teenagers are in the arcade. The bar is the most occupied section and Ramón finds an available bar stool and sits down. He orders a beer from the bartender and guzzles it down in one drink. Fuck all of them, he thinks happily to himself.

"I am tellin you, man. This chick is great. There ain't no one else like her. Even my ma likes her. She could be a little more excitin, but I am working on that."

Ramón looks over at the group of young men sitting together on his right and can't help overhear their conversation. Two of the men are Spanish, and when he looks closely at one, he notices how familiar the young Spanish man with the light brown hair and light brown eyes is to him. I have seen those traits before, he thinks to himself. Catching his stare, the young men look back at him and when Ramón doesn't respond they turn back to their conversation. Except for the light-haired, good-looking Spanish man. He is now staring at Ramón and when Ramón glances over at him again, he realizes exactly who the man is. I just can't get away from any of them, he thinks miserably to himself. One more drink and he would be out of here.

"Ramón, dude, how are ya?"

Rich, that is his name. Sometimes referred to as Richie by his mother. And Lopez was the name of his first stepfather. As interesting as he was, he has no intention of giving his mother's son the time of day.

"Excuse me, do I know you?"

"Know me?" Rich asks. "Dude, we're family. Brothers. I am Rose's son, Rich. When we were all younger we usta visit ya in New York. Don't you remember?"

"No, I don't remember. The mother I had deserted me when I was four. She left me in the care of a useless relative and went back to her own life. She had more children but I was never part of that. She also got married again, but I was not a part of that either."

"Ramón, man, you shouldn't talk about our mother like that."

Rich is beginning to look embarrassed and his friends look uncomfortable.

"Our mother, our mother?" Ramón says. "Rich, I don't know about your mother but my mother was a woman who used phone calls, little presents, phony letters, and phony little family reunions as a way to cover up her guilt. Sure she cared. But she also had her own life, too, and that was what was put first."

"That's not true, Ramón!" Rich shouts. Most of the people at the bar and at the restaurant section are beginning to stare at the two Spanish men arguing over their mother.

"You lived in another state, but she always cared about ya and luved ya. You don't know what life was like for her and for us when our father died and left us with no money! She had to work her ass off! She had to work two jobs just so there was food on the table for us. She was already in a mess of her own. But she always cared about ya, she always luved ya."

"Come on Rich, let's get out of here," one of his friends said to him as they glared at Ramón maliciously. Rich put his hand up and signaled that he was not ready yet.

"Rich, do you know what it is like to go to bed after you have been whipped all over your body? Well, that is what my mother let happen to me. Like I said, she got married, had kids, and then suddenly she becomes like Cinderella! And now she has all this money and starts ignoring me even more. And I don't see one dime of that money, not one dime. Why should she? Why should she give money to the bastard son that she has never cared about! Rich, I don't know about your mother, but mine is a self centered slut who only cares about herself!"

The punch is strong and powerful and it throws him off his barstool and onto the floor. He feels his lip with his hand and feels the blood coming from the cut.

"I'm ready to go now," Rich says to his friends, and they can hear the anger in his voice.

"I'm glad we don't think of you as part of our family."

❧   ❧   ❧

Rose could see the house up ahead and the thought of it filled her with trepidation. She knew the scene before her would not be pretty, but it was something she had to do. She needs release and this is the only way she knows how.

She could have taken her car but the walk would do her good and the time that it takes her to get from her mansion to Shane's house would give her enough time to think about what she will say to her son. As she walks she looks up and notices how the dreary and cloudy June day on this Friday morning is only making her mood more somber. She is just past the fitness center now and from where she is walking on the sidewalk she can make out Shane Daniel's mansion. His house certainly is beautiful. His house, like many other houses in Sandcastles, is designed and constructed in the form of a sandcastle with a roof that is of various lengths and several windows that stick out. The house is of European style with a long chimney that runs up the front. The house is made up mostly of gables, arches, dormers, and a stone-and-stucco exterior. His large and grassy front yard is complimented with several small tiny bushes surrounded by mulch that runs all the way up to the front door. Two gold lamps hang next to the large oak door. She rings the doorbell and waits. What if he is not here? The door opens up suddenly and she is greeted by a handsome man with blonde hair and blue eyes, and around the same age as Rich.

"Can I help you?"

"Hi. Are you Shane? I'm Rose, Rose Fitzpatrick, Ramón's mother."

"Oh yes, hello. That's right, we have spoken on the phone. Nice to meet you. Yes, I am Shane, Shane Daniels. He is in the other room, I will get him for you. Please, come in Rose."

Rose steps in. He is everything that they say he is. Polite, handsome, and nice. She can tell that Shane's house on the inside is just as beautiful on the outside. The floor is made of marble and a mirror sits on the wall off to the right in a gold frame. A large table made out of glass is attached to the wall and holds a vase of flowers. She hears his shoes walking on the floor and watches her thirty-year-old son as he comes from what is obviously the kitchen into the foyer of the house. He is dressed in the clothes required by his employer and Rose can't get over how much he looks like Pedro Santiago, her first husband and Ramón's father. If Pedro wore his black hair long, it would have looked just like Ramón's. Rose can see a little bit of her mother in him and Ramón had the same eye shape as Rose. Rose can also see the injury inflicted by Rich on his mouth.

"I have nothing to say to you."

Rose is expecting these words and had prepared herself greatly for this meeting. He will not make me cry, not this time.

"Ramón, I am not here to fight with you. I am not here to make you do anything. You are a grown man now, not a little boy. I am not here to cause a problem for you."

"Then say what you have to say so I can get back to work. Some of us do have to work around here and don't have rich husbands used for money and security only."

Rose winces. He is so coldhearted. With a disposition just like Pedro. "Ramón, I am here to say that I am sorry. Sorry for what I did to you. You don't know what my situation was like back then, you were too young to understand. You were too young to understand what your father was like. He was abusive, a liar, a womanizer."

"Are you here to talk about my father?"

"I am here to talk about you and your family. Your only family. When I sent you to New York to live I had the best intentions. I couldn't think of any other way. I wanted to let you have the best things in life and the best upbringing. Things I truly believed I couldn't give you. I wasn't getting rid of you. I didn't want you to be involved in the mess I was in. We can't go back in the past anymore. I know what kind of life you had and were having up until the time that you moved back to the Cape. I know everything about you. And I can't take back the years that I wasn't with you or the abuse and pain you went through. We didn't have it easy either, the family that I made with Billy Lopez. I was in just as much of a mess as you were. My kids were in a mess, too. In fact, Rich is still in a mess."

Ramón suddenly laughs.

"I can't change any of those things, Ramón. But one thing that will never change is my love for you. You are right, I should have kept you with me, and I have to live with that for the rest of my life. But I have never stopped loving you. I had every intention of being with you again. Having us all be one happy family. Situations arose and affected all of us. We don't have yesterday, but we do have today. It is not too late. We want you to be part of our family. If you choose to live and act like we don't exist, that is totally up to you. That is your choice. If you want to go and run off and act like you don't have a mother, that is also your choice. But no matter where you go, in my heart and soul I will be loving you and praying for you always."

They are totally silent.

"I have to get back to work."

❧   ❧   ❧

Kristyn grabs her pocketbook from the counter and before she leaves, checks her appearance one more time. She admits that she does look rather good in her white suite with the gold buttons and white scarf wrapped around her neck. She locks the door to the condo and steps out onto the courtyard. Everybody else has left for work and for a moment she believes she is the only person on the courtyard, until she sees her father walk towards her condo. This is it. This is more then she can handle. The memory of last night lingers in her mind and she cannot hold back any longer.

"Kristyn. Are you going to work? My god, do you look beautiful! Aren't you kind of late for work though? Remember what I told you, always be on time for work."

"Dad, I have had enough of this!" She is practically shouting.

He appears to be hurt and confused.

"Enough of what?"

"This whole overprotective attitude, the overprotectiveness that I have been dealing with ever since I was a child!"

"Kristyn, I—"

"Dad, I have been living in this condo for less then two weeks, and I am ready to move out of the state. You have not given me one moment of peace, and I have had it! Especially last night, with Grandma. I had dinner all prepared for Darren and I and you and Grandma came over and wrecked the whole evening. Darren went home early, angry."

"Kristyn, there is something that I don't like about that boy, he is too—"

"Dad, you have said that about every single boy I have ever dated. There is always something wrong with everybody. The reason for this whole condo idea is so I can build my own life away from you and Grandma. I don't want you two over every night. I don't want her to change my condo around, like she used to change my room around. I want my privacy and it is not happening! You have to cut the strings. I am a grown woman, not a child. I don't want to be looked after, doted upon. I want my own life, you are not letting it happen."

They are the harshest words she has ever said to him. His face fills slowly with anger.

"Kristyn, we are your father and grandmother. We only do it because we care about you. We are looking out for your best interests only. Just because you are twenty-two now doesn't mean that we are going to stop looking out for you. If you don't want us in your life anymore, I guess you have made that clear."

He storms away from her and Kristyn watches as he walks out of the court-yard.

❧   ❧   ❧

"So this is where you live?" Justin asks her.

They are inside the condo and Tamie is showing him around. She is glad none of her other friends are home yet. She doesn't want anybody to know about Justin's existence until the time is right. And right now is not a good time.

"When are your friends coming home from work?" Justin asks her as he explores the entire condo.

"They should be home in a while. I am so glad you and I were both able to get out of work early today. We got to spend some time together before the party tomorrow night," Tamie says.

He begins to head towards the stairs.

"Yes, and we both know what is happening soon after the party. What people are going to think of us."

"I don't care what anyone thinks of us. We are no different then anyone else. And we are not greatly related, remember that."

"Is that your room up there?"

When she answers yes, he comes over to her, picks her up, and carries her over his shoulders like a rag doll and heads upstairs.

❧   ❧   ❧

"Can I take your order please?" the male voice asks through the intercom.

Jill has to do all she can do without laughing and tries to speak normally into the Burger King intercom.

"I'll have one cheeseburger, fries, coke, and a Rich Lopez."

"Would you like that Rich Lopez plain or with sweet and sour sauce?"

"Oh, he is already too sweet."

"One Rich Lopez, coming up."

Moments later she has parked her car in the parking lot and he is standing outside her window in his work uniform. He kisses her on the cheek, and she kisses him back.

"I know you aren't going to like it, but when we go out Saturday, do you mind just stopping at Shane's house really quick? We don't have to stay long. He is having a party and really wants me to come. I know you aren't going to be very happy with Ramón there. When I told him you were Ramón's brother, he couldn't believe it. It won't be that bad. People will be mingling. Shane's other friends are really nice, too. Do you mind?"

"No problemo. I don't mind goin there for a little while, because wait until you see the night that I have planned for you, girl!"

❦ ❦ ❦

"You told him off, actually told him off?"

They are sitting at Kristyn's table. He has just come home from work and they are busy planning the rest of their Friday night. She is planning on telling him later on in the evening about the argument she had with her father, but the situation is bothering her and she feels the need to talk about it.

"Yes, I had to. Enough is enough. Especially the stunt he and my grand-mother pulled last night. There was no need for that. I am sure he will tell my grandmother, too. Even though I did it, I feel bad also. I never spoke to him like that ever. I always just accepted his behavior." Beside her at the table, Darren lays his hand lightly on her shoulder.

"It makes you feel bad after you hurt your parents when they were only showing their love in the first place, but you had to do it. You have to make him see that he has to let go of you."

❦ ❦ ❦

Lyle sips his coke and looks up at the large clock that is hung high on the wall of the Cape Cod Mall. Five minutes to nine. Another half an hour and he will leave. On the chair next to him are the various clothing items that he purchased during the evening, as well as a pair of running shoes. He finally decided to himself that if he is going to be stuck on the Cape trying to find Laura, he had better get used to it and start to dress like a Codder. As he finished off the rest of his McDonalds hamburger and drank his Coke, he tortures himself relentlessly and thinks over and over about where she could be. He had found out through an old acquaintance that she had not left the town of Falmouth, but her whereabouts were unknown. As Lyle sips his drink, he examines the reality of his situation. If he had not messed up the way he did back when they went to school together, he would not have had to move to the Cape and build a new life for himself. He certainly was not a Codder and would never feel a part of the environment. But situations had arisen and forced him to undergo dramatic change, and all for the love of his former girlfriend. Lyle looks around the dining area. Rows and rows of tables are clustered together and seat various people of all races, shapes and sizes. On his left and right are small mini-restaurants with long lines of hungry people. Out in the mall, women walk by with clicking high heels, holding various items of purchase. Teenagers walk by in groups of three and four, their Friday night activity found at the Cape Cod Mall. Lyle looks at the activities all around him and pictures Laura holding many shopping bags and hurrying from store to store. He looks at the lines of people standing at the restaurant and when he looks out into the mall again, the scene before him nearly takes his breath away. A woman he immediately recognizes as Laura walks by the dining area with another woman. Laura is holding two bags and the other woman is holding one. Lyle stands up out of his seat so quickly that his Coke and tray of food bang together. The noise startles other customers and they look in confusion as Lyle stares intently at the scene in the mall.

❧   ❧   ❧

"What did you want to do tonight?" Kristyn asks Darren as she goes next to him at the table and gently hugs him. He looks very tired as he glances up at her with a smile.

"Well, we can't do anything too exciting," he says as he winks at her. "We don't want your father to walk in and catch us doing something he would not approve of."

"Forget my father," Kristyn says and their lips meet and kiss for several seconds. When they part, he takes her hand and holds it with his.

"I figured out a way for Lyle and Laura to meet. It is really the best way to do it," Darren says.

"Tell me."

"Tomorrow night at the party we will tell them that we have someone for them to meet. That way, when they see each other, they will think they have been set up on a blind date. They won't know that we know they know each other. We will have them come to the party at separate times. Is that a plan or what?"

"I just hope it works."

He watches Laura walk down the mall and then she disappears into a group of shoppers.

Lyle has left his purchases in the dining area and has forgotten everything except for the woman he is convinced is his ex-girlfriend. He feels incredible excitement in his body and his face is flushed and sweaty. A fat pregnant woman and her male companion push a baby in a carriage and block his view. Up ahead a group of young teenagers walk slow and aimlessly and comment on the stores. Lyle dodges past them and then crashes into a group of elderly women. One of the woman looks at him with scorn in her eyes.

"Watch where you're going, young man. This isn't rush hour traffic!"

Where is Laura? She is suddenly not in sight anymore. Panicked, Lyle runs further up ahead and looks all around him. All he sees are the busy shoppers walking up and down each side of the mall. A store. She must have gone inside a store. Zales Jewelry is on his left. Yes, Laura used to love to browse and look at the jewelry that Lyle could never afford to buy her. He sprints into the jewelry shop and slows his pace down a little as the male manager behind the counter looks at him suspiciously.

The young man running into the jewelry store surprises him and Brian looks away from Karin for a moment. He looks very excited and at the same time bewildered as he walks around the store and seems to look at everything except the jewelry that is in a locked case. Poor guy, Brian thinks to himself, he must have either lost his kid or is trying to find somebody very important to him. Brian turns away from the man and his thoughts turn back to his fiancée.

Karin's face is filled with delight and she is so absorbed in staring at the hooped earrings that she doesn't notice the bewildered man walking around the store. This is their first night out all week and Brian is in the mood to spend some money on her and make her happy, which isn't hard to do. This woman certainly deserves the best treatment, he thinks to himself as he watches her happy expression.

"Brian, they are absolutely beautiful. I love them."

"They will look better on you, that is for sure."

Tears of happiness spring into her eyes and she hugs him quickly.

"I swear I have the best guy around," she whispers in his ear.

"You can wear those earrings to that dinner party next week."

Karin is finished picking out the particular earrings she wants, so Brian signals to the clerk that they are ready.

"I have another surprise coming up real soon. And this will be better then earrings. This surprise will be part of your birthday present," Brian says.

"You're spoiling me," Karin says as she looks happily at the clerk taking the earrings out of the case.

He spots her as she is going into Macy's. From where he is standing he can make out her features, hair, face, and he is convinced even from far away that it is her. The other young woman standing next to her is her good friend Tracey, who she and Lyle had gone out with a number of times. They begin to walk inside the store.

"Laura, Laura! Wait, wait!" he begins hollering and starts sprinting towards Macy's. Just as he is running, a small child shooting a toy water gun squirts him in the eye and Lyle staggers backwards and almost loses his footing. He soon regains his composure and begins to run faster. In the background he can hear a young mother scolding the child.

Laura doesn't seem to notice, but Tracey hears the yelling behind her and turns around. She can't make out his face very clearly, but he is tall with dark hair. And it seems like he is yelling and running towards them very quickly. Some lunatic let loose in the mall.

"Laura, there is some crazy guy running this way. Let's be smart and get out of his way."

Laura looks confused and Tracey grabs her by the arm and they run into the elevator located off to the right at the entrance at Macy's. Tracey hits the button marked down and the doors shut.

❉   ❉   ❉

They are out of Zales now and are leaving the mall. Karin has her earrings boxed up and she is very happily holding onto Brian's hand.

"I can't wait to see what this birthday present is going to be. You have me in suspense now. Is it something that I want?" Karin asks him.

"Something that you have always wanted. Something that I hope you will have for a long time. You will love it, trust me."

❉   ❉   ❉

"Keep your eyes closed. Keep them shut. No peeking!"

It is Saturday morning and he can't think of a better time for her to see her present then right now. They don't have much to do today, and tonight they are going to a party at Curt's friend Shane's house. While Brian is driving the car he instructs Karin to keep her eyes closed with her hand over her eyes as he drives the Cadillac into Sandcastles and through the neighborhoods. They are getting closer and closer and Karin's voice is filled with excitement.

"I can't take the suspense much longer. What did you get me?"

"You shall see, very shortly," Brian says mysteriously.

Brian turns the corner and they are on their street. Up ahead he can see the Cape Cod house. Some major work has been done since his last visit. Both floors are visible and the walls are in and covering each room. Brian parks the Cadillac at the curb.

"Okay, you can open your eyes now."

She takes her hand away from her eyes and she is first filled with confusion and then seconds later delight as she stares at the makings of what will be a beautiful Cape Cod home. Brian can read her thoughts and he knows exactly what to say.

"You always said you wanted to buy land here and build a house, so that is what I did, and soon, this will be our dream home. The Olson family."

Staring at the house with a shocked expression, she gets out of the car and walks as close as she can to the house. They look and admire the work of the carpenters. She yells out screams of happiness and falls into his arms, crying softly.

"You knew, you knew all along that this is what I wanted," she says and then sobs on his chest. She looks lovingly into his eyes.

"I love you," she says to him.

"I love you, too. I have since the night we were introduced."

"This is the best present I ever could have gotten, one I will remember for the rest of my life." Together they hold hands and while they look at the makings of their future home, they decide on the uses of each particular room.

❧   ❧   ❧

"Dianne, telephone. It is the love of your life!"

Dianne is walking up the stairs of the condo and the phone has just rung. Tamie has just come out of the shower and is holding a towel around her naked body. In her hand is the phone. Dianne grins at her wickedly and takes the phone and goes into her bedroom. She knows who the caller is before she says a nervous hello.

"Hi, it's me. What's going on?"

Jon. She knows she can't be wrong.

"Hi. I knew it was going to be you. What are you up to?"

"Nothing much."

There is a brief silence between them and to Dianne it feels like a million years.

"I miss you," Jon says. "We have only been broken up for less than a week, and I miss you already."

"Now, we are not going to say broken-up. We are just taking some time apart, but it doesn't mean that we are through. It is just the best way."

"Are you still going to that party tonight?" Jon asks her, and Dianne knows he is changing the subject.

"Oh, yes, we are all excited. We are all bringing friends. A lot of people from the neighborhood are coming. It'll be fun."

"How about some company?"

Her mind races in a panic. He simply cannot go. Not with Ramón. He will know that Ramon is after her right away. Dianne knows Ramón is on a journey and nothing will stop him.

"I don't think you really have to. It really isn't a big deal. You would probably feel out of place, too, with all those people there."

"Dianne, I know all of your friends. It sounds like you are hiding something from me. Are you?"

"Of course not, but isn't this exactly what we talked about? Not always being together every social event?"

"I don't know. Something doesn't sound right. It sounds like there is something there that you don't want me to see."

"Don't be ridiculous. It is a party with a rich guy, his butler, and his friends."

❦   ❦   ❦

Jill sits on her couch and waits impatiently for Rich to show up. She has fixed herself up tonight and her strawberry blonde hair is pinned up and styled beautifully. Wearing a white summer dress, her face radiates with make-up and her mother has given Jill her white earrings to wear tonight.

"So, where is prince charming tonight?" her mother Christina asks as she leaves the living room.

"Well, right now, he is late, very late. An hour late, actually."

"I don't know. This guy you are seeing is a little too different from you."

Jill looks at her mother, a woman very much resembling her with the same features and strawberry blonde hair, and she can't help believing that she is right. Rich is different, and he is proving it more then ever. Hoping that she can change him, she has an image of him in her mind as being more responsible and more motivated, as well as cleaner and less addictive to a bad lifestyle. Sighing with impatience, Jill walks up to the living room window and then paces. Her mother, who is walking around the living room and waiting for him to show up, has grown impatient, and she has gone into another part of the house. She is suddenly bathed in the glow of his headlights and she looks out the window. Parked in the driveway is his beat up station wagon. Jill hears Rich banging on the driver's side door trying to get out and she laughs and walks to the front door. She hears the door slam and his footsteps as he walks across the driveway. She opens up the door.

"Girl, I am sorry that I am late. Eddie needed a drive to the liquor store, and then there was an old buddy of ours that we ran into, and—"

His eyes light up with surprise.

"Girl, you look fantastic!"

She wishes she could say the same about him. A cigarette sits in his right hand, sending smoke off into the distance. He doesn't look particularly dressed for the date and his jeans have several holes in them.

He seems to notice her disappointment.

"Doesn't your mom want to come out and meet me?"

Jill knows what she will say. How could you go out with somebody like that? "Why don't we get going," she says without any great enthusiasm.

They could have walked. The summer air is warm and relaxing and the stars are shining brightly in the summer sky. Rich insisted that he drive and Jill had to sit in the beat up station wagon for a few minutes while they drove through the neighborhoods of Sandcastles to Shane's mansion. The smell in the car was horrible. All Jill could smell was old paint, rotting metal, and the stench of stale cigarettes. The dashboard had a huge crack and made it difficult for him to see out of. Rich can sense Jill's disappointment and tries to cover it with his humor.

"We'll have fun tonight, afta this party, that is, and this party will seem like a picnic."

They come in through the front door and begin to head out to the back-yard, where the party is being held. Few people are scattered here and there throughout the house and hold alcoholic beverages in their hands while they laugh and talk. Rich lets out a low whistle.

"My brother Ramón sure picked a palace to work in. This pad is mighty fine."

"The upstairs is even prettier."

Although she hates to admit it to herself, the thought of walking around this expensive house with Rich and the way he is dressed makes her feel almost embarrassed. They walk outside and the whole party is before their eyes. His household help, Jillian, a girl in her twenties, Heather, also a young woman, and Donna, a middle-aged woman in her forties, all walk around dressed for the occasion and hold various plates of food and appetizers. There is a long table set up with food and sodas and a huge bucket of ice. A keg of beer sits by the table. The various guests drift around the backyard and walk on the soft grass that feels like velvet. The party drifts all the way over to the pool, and the gate is open with all the guests spilling around it. Shane has put the overhead pool lights on and the glow reflects the expensive clothing of his guests. They notice Ramón, who is standing by the fence and obviously flirting with a mid-dle-aged woman. He turns and stares their way. He gives Jill a slight greeting and barely acknowledges his brother. The laugh and chatter of Shane's guests fills the yard and their glasses clink as they hold them up and drink. Jill notices several of Shane's closest friends and people from the neighborhood who she warmly greets as they pass by.

"How long do we gotta stay here?" Rich asks her. Several of the guests notice Rich and his clothing.

Jill feels very annoyed and doesn't feel like answering him. She sees Shane coming towards her and she looks forward to spending some time with her friend.

❧   ❧   ❧

"Keith, this is my cousin, third cousin, actually, Justin Riley. And Justin, this is my fiancée, Keith Denholm."

She says it quickly and without nervousness. In her mind she knows it is Justin who is giving her the strength to get through this situation.

"Pleasure meeting you."

"Same here."

Justin looks very handsome tonight. He wears a white polo shirt and his hair is combed very neatly. And he is not alone. Another young man accompanies him and Keith also shakes his hand as well.

"This is my friend, Kevin Keneally."

Kevin is a smaller man with brown hair, bluish gray eyes and an Irish complexion. Tamie begins to relax, and only for a little while. So far Keith hasn't noticed a thing and she is beginning to wonder if she is an incredible actress or Keith is just not noticing that there is something greatly wrong with their relationship. She feels as if her stomach is doing somersaults and she begins to feel a little weak. I just can't do this to this man, she thinks to herself. He doesn't deserve this. All these years have gone by and I am throwing him over for my cousin. Tamie looks at Keith's smiling and radiant face and he honestly doesn't think for a second there is something wrong with their relationship. While she is lost in her thoughts, Keith carries on a relationship with the young men. He finds talking to them very easy and while they stand by the fence the time passes as the four of them begin to ease into conversations.

"Tamie, I guess this is a family member you never introduced me to."

"Yes, well, you know Marie, the cousin my mother is close to. This is her son. I was over at the house and told him I was having a party, and being at that age, he wanted to bring a friend and come."

"Yeah, well, young people like parties, typical thing for them to do," Keith says with a laugh and drinks his screwdriver.

Justin realizes it is time to give Tamie a break and he heads over to the sodas and food with Kevin behind him. While they get their food and drinks, Tamie and Keith stand by the fence and relax. Tamie looks into his jovial face and his graying black hair and knows she is doing a terrible thing to him.

❈	❈	❈

Kristyn walks out of the house and Darren walks up to her.

"You look incredible, Miss Coleman," Darren says as he grabs her by the waist and kisses her neck. Kristyn giggles.

"Aren't you glad that you rescued me now?" Kristyn asks him.

"Well, I had the option of just driving past you, but you looked too pretty and helpless, so I stopped."

"Well, thank goodness for March snowstorms," Kristyn whispers lovingly into his face. She looks up at her father, who throws her a disapproving look as he makes his way past the food table. Darren follows her stare.

"Are you two still not speaking?"

"He is speaking to me when he has to. He is still mad though, I can tell."

She forgets her father for a moment and looks at pretty and personable Laura, who is dressed in pink with a pink ribbon in her chestnut hair. She stands by a group of young people and is making conversation with an attractive young man with blonde hair.

"What time did you tell Lyle to come?" she asks Darren.

"I told him a certain time. He suspects nothing. Last night he saw Laura at the mall with that other girl who lives with her. Lyle couldn't get to her in time. I can't wait for his reaction tonight when he sees her."

"It certainly is about time they saw each other."

❈	❈	❈

Dianne needs to get more ice for the cold drinks and she excuses herself from the group of people she is talking to and walks inside the house. The large kitchen is almost in total darkness except for the light over the sink and opening the refrigerator gives her more light to work with. She reaches in and grabs several ice trays and lays them on the counter. When she lays the last one on the table, she closes the refrigerator door and then stares into the face of Ramón. He has surprised her and come right up to her without being noticed. He wears a slight grin and his eyes burn passionately. The darkness almost makes him look glowing, Dianne thinks to herself, and she realizes that this moment has been coming for a while. Suddenly, she is confused about her feelings for John and the recent events that have made her question her life. The same questions always arise. Where is she going and with whom is she going? Yet he stands there in his dark black jacket and coal black eyes studying her and the sexual feeling bursts out of her.

"You shouldn't be caught in a dark room with all the lights off. You don't know what you will find," he says. He talks in the sexiest whisper.

"And you shouldn't be going up behind strange girls and scaring them either," is her reply.

He laughs in the still of the room.

"Oh, I can't help it this time. Being in this room with you, I thought I would take some ice and cool myself off. Put out the fire in me."

Dianne suddenly has no idea what she is doing and she can't resist when Ramón grabs her and starts kissing her passionately on the mouth. To Dianne, it seems as if they kiss forever and as he is yanking the buttons on her shirt and trying to free them, she is slowly undressing him with her left hand. Suddenly she stops. They can't do this. Not here. Somebody will walk in on them. Ramón is now lifting her off the floor and onto the white countertop. He sees the trays of ice and hurls them onto the floor as he lunges at her. She grabs him by the arms and stops him.

"We can't do this here," she says. "Somebody will walk in on us."

"Let them walk in on us," Ramón says, out of breath and panting. "They can watch and take lessons."

Jill sits on the torn and dirty couch. She never wanted to go home more than right now. Her night of fun at Shane's house and then with Rich afterward has turned into a complete disaster and she almost feels like crying. She looks at Rich who is sitting next to her on the couch. Laughing uncontrollably, his shirt is completely off and his pants are unbuttoned. A small table sits in front of him with an ashtray that is filled with cigarettes. Empty beer bottles are on the table and they roll over and bang together. Jill looks around the room and at the other occupants and she now realizes that people of his kind all hang together. Eddie sits on a couch directly opposite to their couch and his eyes are glassy and red and he holds a cigarette and a can of beer. Rich's two other friends are the most interesting. One is a fat and greasy girl about Jill's age with spiked hair and a rough complexion. She holds the hand of her boyfriend Dwight, a tall man with a shaved head and a long and unkempt goatee. He also smokes a cigarette and is consuming a number of beers. Although he is holding his girlfriend Patty's hand, his curious eyes are fixed on Jill and every so often he turns to stare at her. Jill looks at Rich and she can't believe he is doing this to her. She also realizes that his big plans for the evening have not been realized. The nightmare began at Shane's house. Jill should of known that Rich with his clothing and his wild lifestyle would never fit in with Shane and Shane's friends, and while Jill socialized with different people, Rich looked bored and completely out of place. It was no surprise also that Ramón and Rich would tolerate each other but not talk to each other after their brawl at the Sandbar. After an hour and a half, she knew it was time to leave. Rich was showing signs of complete boredom and was signaling to her that he wanted to leave, so Jill said her goodbyes and they left. She felt bad because she wanted to stay, and Shane looked disappointed that she was leaving. She also saw Shane talk with a young blonde woman the whole time, and if Shane got his way, she would be his lucky hit for the evening. Now here they sat, in the strange apartment of Eddie's friend Dwight. With the exception of Jill, all three of them were having a wonderful time of talking, laughing, and acting very obnoxious. Rich drank beer after beer and then burped so loudly and suddenly he had the three of them with tears in their eyes from so much laughing. Dwight's girlfriend Patty made no attempt to talk to her and Jill figured the reason for this was they had nothing to say to each other. Jill tried to make conversation with Rich and show she was having a good time, but Rich blew smoke in her face and constantly pressured her into consuming alcohol. He kept asking her if she was having fun, because he was. Rich got up off the couch and stumbled into the bathroom and shut the door. They heard a loud thud as he fell to the floor, and his friends started laughing. Jill can't take it any more and she gets up and runs out of the apartment.

❧   ❧   ❧

Lyle locks the door to his condo and walks out onto the courtyard. After the scene at the mall when he lost Laura at Macy's, and the heartbreak of losing her once again, attending this party is the last way in which he wants to spend his Saturday evening. He walks off the courtyard and past the adjoining condos and soon he is on the grass and cutting through the small patch of woods that leads to the party. Off in the distance he can hear the voices of many people and the sounds of faint music. The only real reason he has for coming to this house is the blind date set up by Kristyn and Darren. The thought does not thrill Lyle in the least. I will do it for Darren, but I won't get any fun and enjoyment out of it, and I know I will have no interest in her at all, he thinks to himself. He assumes that the party is being held outside, so he travels through the strange house that he has never been in before and then he is at the deck that leads to the backyard. Off in the distance he sees a large Olympic-size pool with people talking and laughing around it. He sees a great many people with food and drinks and soft rock music comes from a tall speaker in the corner of the yard. If the woman he is set up with is here at this party, she must be hiding very well, Lyle thinks miserably to himself. Then suddenly he sees Kristyn and Darren coming up to him. Darren wears a look of embarrassment and Lyle knows exactly what he is going to say before the words leave his mouth.

"Lyle, what's up man? We're glad that you're here. We have some bad news for you though. Kristyn and I are very sorry about it. We did have a date set up for you, but before you came over, this girl, a friend of Kristyn's, was shacking up with another group of people and there was a guy she was interested in, and they got cozy, and, and—"

Lyle finishes the sentence for his friend. "Took off and now I don't have a date waiting for me anymore."

"Lyle, we are wicked sorry, really," Kristyn says. "We know we probably dragged you out of your house for nothing. We tried to tell her to stay, but she had other interests tonight. While you are here, though, try and have some fun. We are all having a great time, and my uncle and his friends are a great bunch to hang out with."

I'm sure Laura is having a great time, too, somewhere where I don't know where she is, as well as the other girl who just left here, Lyle thinks to himself.

❁   ❁   ❁

"What's the matter, haven't you ever gone skinny dipping before?"

Ramón is standing by his bedroom window and looking down at the pool. From under the covers of his bed Dianne watches him as the light from the moon reveals his naked body. She contemplates the idea he has just put forth and tries to weigh her decision in the drunk stages of her mind. Everything is so hazy, she thinks to herself, and for the time being she has put rationalization and responsibility for her actions in the back of her mind. She has even forgotten about what in her heart she knows is going to betray her relationship with Jon. But, she can't resist him any longer and he has totally succeeded in the manipulation of her soul. They had managed to get off the kitchen table without being greatly physical and for the entire rest of the night he didn't let her out of his sight for seconds at a time. They were careful to keep their lust away from Shane and everybody else, and now that it is after midnight and the party is over they are able to steal away and have privacy. During the evening Dianne had let the alcohol help her escape from the realities of Jon, and the confusion about where her life was going. She knows she has gone too far now. She had never drank this much in her entire life. He has just mentioned going down to the pool and taking a swim, and to Dianne the idea both excites her and thrills her. He turns his head away from the window and looks at her lying naked in his bed.

"Come on, it will be safe. Trust me. I know, I work here. No one is around, the party is over. Your friends have all gone home, and don't worry about Shane. Shane is not going to find out, believe me. He got lucky with that blonde girl tonight and he is off somewhere with her." He finally has her convinced and they go down the stairs without any fear. No one has turned the pool lights off and at this hour of the early morning the light gives off a glow and the awaiting pool seems to call out to them and invite them. They step over empty beer bottles and food and make their way inside the gate of the pool. He grabs her and kisses her passionately and she slowly undresses him once again and soon he is free of his clothing. He undresses her in the same way and then they embark upon their adventure. As the moon shines upon them, they dive into the crystal clear blue water and let the invigorating feeling refresh them and put them at ease. Dianne has forgotten everything in her life that matters except for this daring and bold Spanish man she is completely falling for. Ramón goes up the ladder of the long Olympic pool, the diving board, and Dianne laughs as he goes to the end of the diving board and does a double flip in the water.

"I should have known what you were planning!" a voice yells out in the darkness.

Dianne freezes and seems to forget all sense of time and place until the voice becomes familiar to her and she turns around and gasps. Jon is standing on the cement and is coming closer and closer to them. His face is full of rage and betrayal, and Dianne can tell by his voice that he has consumed a great deal of alcohol before coming over here.

"You whore! I should have known all along. I should of known you weren't telling the truth about this place on the phone. We are through, you hear that? We are through, you conniving piece of trash whore!" he shouts as loud as he can.

Dianne freezes in the water and can't seem to move a muscle to act. The alcohol and the shock has her in a trance. Ramón gets out of the pool quickly and throws on his pants that are lying on the cement. While Ramón makes sense out of the situation, Jon continues to shake with rage and scream obscenities at Dianne.

"No problem, man. No problem. We were just having a little fun. Everything is cool," Ramón says.

"Relax?"

The sight of him and Ramón's words suddenly startle Jon and now he is completely transfixed on Ramón. Dianne feels tears in her eyes and the shock of her naked body in this situation suddenly makes her start to sob as she treads water.

"You!" Jon shouts, "I'm going to kill you. You come and just take my girl-friend away."

Jon lunges for Ramón, and now Dianne's gasp turns into a chilling scream as Jon grabs hold of Ramón and punches him in the face! Suddenly Dianne's sense of reality comes back and the things that are important to her are right before her eyes. The terror before her is making the alcohol evaporate in her body and she is seeing what she should have seen coming all night long. Ramón recovers from the attack and with the blood streaming down his face from his cut lip, he shakes Jon with his hands and throws him in the water with all his clothes on! Ramón's rage seems to come out of him and Dianne swears that he takes all the anger and hatred he has for other people in his life out on Jon, and Jon's body feels the powerful and strong blows of Ramón. Dianne now has the ability to move forward and she starts yelling for the two men to stop as she swims quickly over to them. Jon's face is full of terror as he fights the out-of-control Spanish man and he swims over to the side and gets out of the pool. Ramón chases after him and when Ramón is on the cement also, a punch is thrown that sends one of the men crashing into the steel ladder at the side of the pool. The man's head hits the ladder and his body falls to the ground after the strong and powerful blow. Blood spurts from the wound and leaks onto the cement. Dianne screams in pure terror and she has totally forgotten her drunken state as she makes her way over to the man as the other shocked man joins her.

The man is greatly wounded and Dianne feels for a pulse. In her panic she has forgotten her nakedness and doesn't even care. She checks for a pulse and there is none. The man isn't moving! The reality of the horror sinks in and Dianne believes this man might very well be dead.

❧   ❧   ❧

Kristyn is still in her nightgown as she looks out the window at the beautiful sunny Sunday morning and then suddenly the doorbell rings. She glances over at her bedroom door that is shut and thinks about who is in it and then answers the door.

"Dad. What are you doing here?" she asks as she nervously looks at her bedroom door. Bill Coleman stands before her and his face is filled with apologies and forgiveness. "Hi, pumpkin, I just want to come in and talk to you," he says sweetly. "I have been doing a lot of thinking and you and I need to sit down and have a nice long father and daughter chat, just the two of us."

"Dad, this really is not a good time to chat right this second, I —"

"No, I insist. I feel I must get this off my chest because it bothers me. How about putting on a cup of coffee for your old man? We can go get ourselves some donuts just like on Sunday mornings when you were little, don't you remember, Kris?"

Kristyn lets him in and feels panicked as she looks at her bedroom door. "Well, let's talk in the living room, it'll be better, and—"

She never finishes the sentence because the door to her bedroom opens up and Darren comes out of her room naked except for his underwear. He has not heard the doorbell ring or Bill's voice due to deep sleep and is now very confused as he looks at Kristyn and Bill for an explanation about what is going on.

"So, are we really alone?" Tamie asks Justin as they fall on his bed together and hold each other's hands.

"Yeah, my parents won't be around here. We have the whole place to ourselves, the whole beach to ourselves, no one to bother us, to judge us."

"No one to even look at us," Tamie says happily and kisses his cheek.

"The only ones looking will be us at each other," Justin says as they look into each other's eyes and then kiss. Justin gets up off his small bed and opens the window so the warm summer morning drifts into his room.

"Let's go walking on the dunes tonight," Tamie says.

An incredible feeling comes over both of them and soon they are grabbing at each other and kissing each other with a great deal of force. Tamie unbuttons Justin's shirt and takes it off as her shirt comes off and they both continue kissing.

"What the hell is going on here?" Tamie hears a male voice ask and their discovery of one another becomes an act of pure guilt. Tamie and Justin look up in horror as Marie, Justin's stepfather, and Keith come walking into Justin's bedroom and stare at the two of them.

Tracey is sleeping very late today and Laura is dressed up with nothing to do until the afternoon when she is going to her parents' house in Falmouth for a cookout. She looks very pretty in pink shorts, pink top, sandals, and her chestnut hair combed to perfection. She walks around the condo looking for something to do and feeling very bored, she decides to go for a walk around Sandcastles for some exercise and refreshment. She can browse around the general store, walk the streets and check out the new bakery that is being built at Sandcastles. The day certainly is gorgeous and when she walks outside she notices how blue the sky is. Not a cloud can be found. She glances over at Shane's mansion and thinks about what a fun time she had last night and how meeting a young man there with his friends had made the whole night. She and the young man were very attracted to each other and after they went off last night during the party, he promised to call her. She also felt a little rude about leaving because Kristyn and her boyfriend had suggested that she meet somebody they were bringing but Laura had gotten distracted during the party and plans changed. Usually blind dates never worked out and god knows what kind of a man they were introducing her to. Laura also thought she heard an ambulance going down the streets and past the condos and she hadn't heard about anybody getting sick or injured yet today. As she is walking down the courtyard, one of the condos on the right opens up suddenly and a young man comes out in very expensive summer clothes, shuts and locks the door to his condo, and heads out to the parking lot. At first, Laura doesn't think anything of it until she gets closer to the man who is walking and he turns and looks in her direction. When he does she freezes and her heart begins pounding. They walk closer and closer to each other and suddenly they both recognize each other.

❧   ❧   ❧

He picks the cellular phone up from the passenger side of the Cadillac and dials her phone number. She is probably eagerly awaiting my phone call, Brian thinks to himself with a smile. He sure did have a great girlfriend. Up ahead, the traffic on Route 25 heading toward the Bourne Bridge is light and Brian knows he will be home very soon. One ring, two rings.

"Hello?"

"Hi. You knew it was me. Why did you even have to ask?"

"Well, it could have been my other fiancée calling me."

"Many fiancées, only one house at Sandcastles."

"Oh, my house, I can't wait to move in. How soon?"

"It could even be ready before the wedding."

"Oh, I can't wait. How was your day today, did you see the kids from your old neighborhood in Warwick?"

"Yes, I saw all the old friends. It's so good because even though I live on the Cape now I always know my old friends from Warwick will still be there."

"Listen, I have a call on the other line, so I have to hang up. I'll call you when I get out of work tomorrow, okay?"

"I love you."

"Love you, too."

He hangs up and suddenly the Bourne Bridge is in sight. As he begins to drive up it he marvels at how fast he got home from Warwick. Suddenly a long tractor trailer truck heading in the other direction crosses the strip of grass that separates the two highways and heads right at Brian. Brian screams in terror and turns the wheel quickly to avoid getting hit head on by the gigantic truck.

To be continued …

978-0-595-44825-8
0-595-44825-9

Printed in the United States
91119LV00004BA/676-714/A